T0356992

GL●RIA

GLORIA

A Novel

●

Andrés Felipe Solano

Translated from the Spanish by
Will Vanderhyden

Counterpoint
California

GLORIA

This is a work of fiction. All of the characters, organizations, and events portrayed in this novel are either products of the author's imagination or are used fictitiously.

First Counterpoint edition: 2025

ISBN: 978-1-64009-685-1

The Library of Congress Cataloging-in-Publication data is available.

Jacket design by Farjana Yasmin
Jacket image: Untitled, *ca. 1970 by Garry Winogrand © The Estate*
of Garry Winogrand, courtesy Fraenkel Gallery, San Francisco
(image has been cropped with the permission of the Winogrand Estate)
Book design by Wah-Ming Chang

COUNTERPOINT
Los Angeles and San Francisco, CA
www.counterpointpress.com

Printed in the United States of America

10 9 8 7 6 5 4 3 2 1

GL●RIA

SHE HAS NEVER SMOKED AND MAY NEVER LIGHT UP A cigarette, but today, which I decide to imagine bright and bustling, she should, she should take advantage of her boyfriend being late to slowly inhale the smoke, aware of how her lipstick is leaving a mark on the filter, the nervous pressure of her lips giving it a slightly oval shape. Inside that silvery blue cloud of smoke, the wait is less agonizing, more bearable, as they say of certain afflictions, because that's what it is, a disquiet she discovered upon waking that morning, earlier than usual, when the light slipped softly in through her room's window and she couldn't yet hear animals knocking over bottles on that street corner in Queens. When she first opened her eyes, she'd even felt hopeful, reentering the world without fear. It usually takes her a little while to come to terms with what it is to be alive and awake, a few minutes to tentatively break the waters of sleep, but today is different, because today is a day that should last forever—that is, if Tigre ever bothers to show up. The feeling of disquiet, far from receding, became a stabbing pain in her chest that, as the hours passed, under the spray of the shower, eating the one piece of toast she had for breakfast, calling Tigre to arrange where to meet, swelled into an irrepressible stormy sea, rising furiously through her whole body. So now the best thing she can do is smoke. Yet let's suppose—because that's also what this is about, supposing. We suppose, then, that Tigre doesn't like smelling nicotine in the folds of her polka-dot blouse, in her chestnut hair, in her eyelashes, curled with the aid of a device purchased the previous week, after her shift at the photo lab. And to dispel the issue, she had made a deal with him. Yes, a deal, knowing that he would never hold up his end. Fine, I'll quit smoking if you start showing up on time, she said. A laugh in response, a laugh like an empty can of crackers rolling down a long staircase. That laugh and showing up late and a volatile temperament and wide-collared shirts are the defining characteristics of Tigre, a nickname he earned in a legendary fight, he told her as they walked through Manhattan on one of their first dates. In fact, that's how he'd introduced himself months before. Nice to meet you, Tigre, he said, smiling and confident in a parking ramp, in a vague imitation of those young fighter pilots she saw as a girl on the screen of a damp-walled movie theater in the small city where she was born. And as he did so, as he said the nickname that'd become a permanent stand-in for his real name, Tigre reached out his large, white, hairy-fingered hand to take her slender, white, long-fingered hand. A minute later, they were in the van that would take them to Niagara Falls. But that was last year, at the end of autumn, and now we're in a diner in the middle of the spring of 1970, at 4:25 p.m., and he's nowhere to be seen. From one moment to the next, she feels disgusted by the smoke, by the smell, like how sometimes, bored of a beach or a mountain, she turns her back on it without any regret. I suggest she leave the cigarette half smoked. She does so. She stubs it out slowly, firmly, sitting at a table beside the window, watching people pass by outside, a table where she's been waiting for Tigre for an hour, maybe less. *La Mallor-qui-na*, she reads, separating the syllables, on the side of the hexagonal ashtray, before saying to herself, how strange, he's never been this late. Almost an hour now, maybe more. The seed of disquiet, discovered in the center of her chest when she got up that morning, has grown into a tangled mess of tachycardia and burning palm trees. And it's not helping to have an old man leering at her from the opposite corner of the establishment. Dominican? Puerto Rican? Cuban? It must be the red miniskirt, but how could she not wear it, it fits so well and she'd been saving it for weeks, months, for that day, for today.

She lifts her right arm that, bored, she'd left dangling under the table, and looks at her watch again. Her mother gave it to her a week before she boarded the plane to the United States. It's one of the few things she brought with her. She's placed a strange faith in it, a certainty common for others but not for her. A faith that her mother really does love her, despite the fact that everything she does demonstrates the opposite. The first and worst was having sent her when she was seven years old to the capital to attend a boarding school full of varicose nuns. The last, not having come to El Dorado Airport to see her off. Let's see: 4:32 p.m. She would insult him if she could, the problem was that, with Tigre, the insults never came, it was as if she'd stashed them in a box and when she opened it to use them, they weren't there. Just an empty box, smelling of wood shavings and dust, a dead insect inside, a ladybug devoid of color, a box like the ones in the ironing room of her family's enormous home in Bogotá. She's ready to remember it, to go down the stairs, sensing the ghost in her belly, the house is haunted, to glimpse her reflection out of the corner of her eye in the quartz crystal mirror hanging in the living room, to pass through the dining room with eight place settings, to enter the kitchen, to walk across it and out onto the patio to greet the toucan that her mother's friend brought them from the Amazon, but before she can, she's seized by that very particular fear that's overcome her every so often since she's been in New York. Because so far, it's only happened to her in New York, never in Missouri, where she spent a few months she'd considered unforgettable but no longer were, not after confronting the resounding roar of the city. The only city. The thing is, she's come to believe that, suddenly, without warning, she'll forget something simple, fundamental, at moments such as this, reading the hands on her watch in La Mallorquina diner, waiting for Tigre, who's nowhere to be seen, fucking hell. Or frying an egg. Her name. Things like that. Last week she even felt like she was going to wake up someday having forgotten how to play ping-pong. She's been thinking about it and is sure that in another time, in another place, that fear would've wrecked her. It would've paralyzed her, prevented her from even pulling up her stockings in the morning. There, on those electric streets where even the rumble of parading taxis and the howls of the people excited her, never, not a chance. If the sacrifice for being here is to forget everything and learn it all over again, I'm ready to accept it. She's surprised by how calmly she says it. She didn't know you could have a feeling like this for a city, that you could long for it the way she's begun to long for New York, though it might also be because her mother isn't there and not just because of the musical rattle of the subway platforms, the magazines in that new language she already finds herself thinking in once or twice a day, the shop windows that change weekly, the way life should change, the men and their newfound beauty, her stable Friday paycheck, and her new addiction—pizza. What a strange food, so simple yet so perfect. She'd never seen anything like it in Bogotá. She'd eaten hamburgers at Crem Helado de la Treinta y Dos with her sisters, sure; never pizza. She tried it on her landlady's recommendation and now it's all she eats. Cheese, with a sprinkle of oregano, and that's it. They already know her at John's, on the corner of Grand Avenue and Haspel Street. They see her come in and before she sits down at the bar, they have a slice served up on a piece of wax paper. Being young in that city, making connections with people, smiling at them, having them smile at her, hating them, having them hate her. Let's see: 4:39 p.m., 4:40! The hands seem to have begun to accelerate. She calculates. She goes over the subway stops to Madison Square Garden. She's already memorized all of the F Line stops down to Midtown. In a taxi, not a chance, at that time of day, they would never get there on time and it would end up costing a lot. Tigre had twenty minutes to show up or they wouldn't get in. Not one minute more. And if they didn't get in, she would find those lost insults. Or invent some new ones if she had to. New insults invented for Tigre and Tigre alone.

"Hey, shouldn't you be in line already?"

The voice startles her, a voice she hears almost every day. In general, it's a voice that helps her relax, makes her feel safe, a lighthouse in a stormy sea, but she wasn't prepared to hear it in that diner and at such close proximity. Amparo has the bad habit of close talking. Luckily, she doesn't have bad breath. When had she come in? If she hadn't asked for the day off, the two of them would've left the lab together and walked to the salon where her friend worked a five-to-nine shift. Two jobs, three if you counted the people she saw at home on Sundays. Amparo's mother is bedridden, which was why she couldn't go to the concert. They live alone, opposing mirrors replicating each other infinitely, in an apartment near LaGuardia, full of tables covered with embroidered tablecloths, smelling of cheap powders and desiccated drool, where she visited them two weeks ago and they drank hot chocolate as if they were living in a mountain town in Colombia and had just come home from mass. La Sola, that's Carlota's nickname for Amparo. Ehhh, hanging out with la Sola again? Carlota called her la Sola until one day, in the middle of Roosevelt Avenue, she asked her to, please, stop. Hearing the nickname, she couldn't help but think of a white tapeworm—*una solitaria*—like the one that had emerged from the rectum of one of her boarding-school classmates in the middle of the night. The daughter of Our Dear President, the mother superior repeated annoyingly every time she referred to that fragile and ugly girl, all bones, a heron-girl from a *llanera* song. She remembers how she accompanied the sobbing girl to the bathroom so she could finish passing the worm without the embarrassment of the nuns and everyone else finding out. In the end, the worm escaped the toilet and wound up stranded on the cold tiles, writhing in the moonlight. That's the kind of memory she has of the boarding school her mother sent her to. Intestinal parasites and an inexplicable fear of the Colombian flag. If she passes by a really big one, she's overwhelmed by the feeling that it's going to wrap around her and swallow her whole.

"I'm waiting for Tigre."

"Ah, Tigre. You and your Tigrecito . . ." Amparo says, still standing.

There's a contemptuous, even argumentative, tone when she says his name. When Amparo uses diminutives, and she often does, there's usually a hint of warmth, but now she's not so sure. She's been a little hostile since she told her in the locker room that she was going to see Him in concert. So silly, she thought in that moment, so silly she repeats to herself now, gesturing for her to sit. If she hadn't, Amparo would've stood there until she turned gray, she's one of those women who believe certain formalities help prevent existential collapse. She doesn't know her that well, maybe that means they're just work friends, not being able to anticipate her reactions. She thought Amparo would've been surprised, the way her sisters were when she called to tell them from one of the phone booths at Jackson Heights subway station. Their jubilation on the other end of the line was infectious and only then did she really comprehend the true dimension of what she was going to experience on Saturday, that is, today, April 11, 1970. Oh, that's nice, was all Amparo said when she'd told her in the locker room.

Amparo pulls back the chair she'd indicated and sits down for a chat, while pushing back her long red hair, which gets washed out every summer. Under the lights in the photo lab, she doesn't look this haggard, and might easily pass for much younger than her actual age, which is forty. Carlota doesn't understand this either, how she's befriended a woman twice her age. The thing is that Amparo is as loyal as an echo.

"Tomorrow, right? At four. Try to think of something he liked and bring it if you can. It could be a food or a drink," Amparo says.

The concert had occupied her mind for days and she hadn't remembered that tomorrow, Sunday, she was supposed to go to Amparo's apartment for a formal session. She hadn't told anybody what she hoped to do, especially not her mother, when she called her a couple days ago and her mother let slip: *seventeen years ago today, your father was* . . . She always trailed off at that point, unable to utter the most terrible verb of all. Her friend is a medium and has promised to contact her father. Amparo's mother had been a witch back in Colombia, but a more powerful witch had waged a war against her, in the countryside and the cities, and she'd been forced to flee and come live in the United States with her daughter. The battle left her mother debilitated and weakened, but not beaten. Amparo inherited some of her powers, among them the ability to commune with the dead. That's why she'd gone to drink hot chocolate at Amparo's apartment. She wanted to hear in detail, away from eavesdropping coworkers, how and when Amparo was going to contact him, her father. Was it possible for her to miss him even though she was barely three years old when he was buried? Yes, it was possible. Sometimes a future that never took shape weighs more heavily than any past.

Amparo stares at the cigarette butts in the ashtray without judgment and begins humming a song, a kind of olive branch, an all is forgotten, a let's be work friends again. She starts out quietly and only when the song imposes itself over the conversations at the other tables does she recognize it. It's an old one, but it's one she likes. She starts humming along and then adds the lyrics. Soon they find themselves singing the tango she'd heard walking hand-in-hand with her widowed mother, her jewelry jingling, past one of the little cafés of her childhood, where tie-wearing men drunkenly embraced each other in the full light of day and every so often a bottle of aguardiente slid off the table and crashed to the floor. Now she's the one leading, imitating the deep voice of Sarita

Montiel . . . *Fumando espero al hombre a quien yo quiero, tras
los cristales de alegres ventanales* . . . A tall and slender waiter
appears, and they get embarrassed by their spontaneous musical outburst. They fall silent and the remnants of the song
disperse in her mind, tatters of burning paper . . . *Mientras
fumo mi vida no consume porque flotando el humo me suele ador-
mecer.* Amparo orders a café con leche and then reaches out a
hand to softly touch the hem of her red miniskirt. From the
expression on the face of the old man in the corner—Haitian?
Venezuelan? Colombian like them?—he appears to envy her.
Amparo nods, indicating that she approves of the finish. She
tells Amparo about Alexander's, a department store she discovered last week in Manhattan. We should go together, she
says, afraid of going overboard. Her friend smiles without a
hint of bitterness and says yes, one of these days, when she has
something to spend. I'm poor here, but I wasn't born poor,
let's keep that clear, Amparo often repeats in the locker room.
From rector of a girl's school to machine operator. A house
of her own in Colombia for her younger siblings and rent-
ing an apartment in a run-down building near LaGuardia,
where you hear planes land every five minutes and the windows vibrate. She's a machine operator too, they work side by
side, but the word *poverty* doesn't even enter her mind. Maybe
because it's all an adventure and New York hasn't knocked
her down yet. Not yet. For now, there's just too much litter

on the sidewalks. The blackout, the rats' nests, the burning buildings, and the sex epidemic are far away. And anyway, her mother lives in a mansion with four employees and a ton of Meissen porcelain and she works as a machine operator at the Agfa photo labs, so what does that make her exactly? She doesn't know.

The café con leche arrives steaming, without the milk skin having formed. Amparo smiles at the waiter and, to keep him there a few seconds longer, orders a mallorca, the Puerto Rican sweet roll that gave the place its name. She's always angling for attention and has nice teeth and prominent breasts, but the excess eye makeup, two raccoon stripes, scares off most prospects. She doesn't dare tell her, knowing that being single for a while has made Amparo sensitive to such comments.

"Plain mallorca," the waiter responds without returning Amparo's smile. She comes out in support of her friend, offering a safety net in the form of a question, a question that, without being aware of it, will end up triggering a horrible memory that'll accompany her the rest of the time she spends waiting for Tigre to appear.

"And Mr. Murray? Is he okay?"

Mr. Murray is their boss. His son had an accident—if you can call drinking a bottle of Baygon an accident—and he hadn't come into work the day before.

"Yes, he's okay. They pumped his son's stomach, and it didn't lead to anything serious," Amparo says, taking three little sips of her coffee. Then she leaves it on the table and doesn't touch it again.

"But that doesn't matter. I almost forgot. Guess what. They came for the pictures. Mr. Murray's secretary told me," she adds, widening her eyes and slapping the table with the palm of her hand. The spoons and ashtray jump, the coffee almost spills, and she thinks that the shadow of revenge is once again hovering over them, why else would Amparo want to ruin her afternoon by bringing that up now? She hadn't thought about what had happened for a while and now it would be hard to get it out of her head.

Amparo suddenly grabs ahold of her wrist and looks at her watch.

"Ten to five! I have to go. I'll tell you all about it tomorrow at my place. Eat the mallorca, they're really good here. And have fun at the concert."

Amparo stands up, smooths her skirt, gives her a quick kiss on the cheek, and leaves, waving to her all the way across the restaurant until she's out the door. She watches her pass in front of the window, smiling, not really understanding why, it's impossible that four hours of washing strangers' hair would make her happy. She lets the doubt spread further to avoid thinking about what Amparo had said and asks the waiter to clear the café con leche. She hesitates to take a bite of the powdered-sugar-dusted mallorca. She's hungry, but not that hungry. If she does, she'll have to eat the whole thing, and if she doesn't, it's possible they'll serve it to someone else. The worst would be for them to throw it away without anyone having touched it. It's inescapable. It starts with those words: Guess what? They came for the pictures. They came. That was exactly what she'd said. They came, instead of he came. The man who took the pictures and one of the women? Two men? Or was it an indistinct they came; a they came that was really a he came? Just one. It's Tigre's fault, if he'd shown up sooner, they would be talking about where they were going to meet Carlota or at least fighting about why he was so late. So, to avoid contemplating the absolute tragedy, the misery, the meaninglessness of her life if they got there and the doors were closed, she decides to think about what had happened at the Agfa lab. She does so with legs crossed, sitting sideways in her chair, slightly back from the table she'd specifically picked out so she could see when Tigre arrived. She finds herself ready to examine the incident with renewed attention, a cool head, now that she has more time and isn't being ambushed by those images, walking alone in a park or down the aisles of a supermarket. She hasn't told Tigre anything about it, of course. The vileness of the whole story hasn't faded, touching her to later drift away and disappear into the New

York sewers. Just the opposite. It's taken up residence deep inside her, entangling her soul, and she's terrified that somebody might find it. Or at least that's what I think.

Last Monday, she arrived at eleven o'clock, punched in, left her purse in her locker, and greeted Amparo. After a quick hug and kiss on the cheek, regarded with suspicion by their gringo coworkers, she walked with her lab coat, gloves, and safety glasses to the cutting room. It was a warehouse similar to a sports coliseum, transversed by iron beams, white lights hanging from the ceiling, and hundreds of machines lined up in rows. Hers was in a corner, against a wall, not far from the bathroom. Before turning it on, she always ran a finger across her name, stitched in red into the thick fabric of her lab coat. Gloria. A vote of confidence, a superstition picked up along the way, to keep the machine functioning properly. It was better than praying to the Virgin of Guadalupe, to the Virgin of Charity of Cobre, or to Our Lady of Luján, like the other Latin American women who worked as operators did. For the others, there was no need. Carol, Loretta, or Sue wouldn't have their pay docked if the pedal on their machine got damaged and they couldn't complete their eight-hour shift. She turned hers on and started cutting slides as she'd done so many other mornings since she'd gotten that position. For the first few minutes, she was overcome by a feeling like that of traveling. In the least expected moment, among the predictable family photos of backyard cookouts, couples at graduation dances, or birthday cakes, she knew that she would find a sailor in some Asian port or a plumed singer in a Caribbean nightclub. That was why she liked her job, apart from the paycheck, it allowed her to imagine other lives, dozens of lives, to not be confined to her own. It was true that sometimes she had to cut some slightly mysterious photographs, like a series of hunchbacked or openly terrifying women, or like that collection of witchcraft objects, dolls with dirty faces, unfamiliar saints, and teeth scattered across a purple cushion, but nothing had prepared her to see what she saw when she came back to the cutting room after eating a tuna sandwich in the cafeteria. The section chief, Mr. Murray, had told her in person to come by Human Resources at the end of the afternoon. They were extending her contract. She'd been waiting for this news all week; if it hadn't come, she would've had to go back to nannying. She'd stopped because she'd been creeped out by the baby of a German couple who wouldn't stop staring at her. Or she would have to go to the pajama factory where she'd been offered a job sewing elastic bands into pants for fifty cents an hour. She didn't know which would be worse. Before getting hired at Agfa, she'd even inquired at a butcher shop on Elmhurst if they

needed someone. The owner sent her to his wife's beauty salon to get a job washing hair, explaining that she wouldn't last
a day among the men with knives and chain mail. She hadn't
bothered. She wasn't like Amparo. She preferred bloody
water to other people's hair. Out walking one morning, she
went into the photo lab and, with the conviction of someone
asking at a hardware store if they sold bread, asked the secretary if they had any openings. They interviewed her that
same day at an oval table big enough for twenty people. She
explained who she was, where she came from, and what she
wanted. In those years, it wasn't a problem to be Colombian.
Or Mexican, or Argentinian. Welcome, Ms. Mendoza, you
start Monday. And she'd been there for six months without
ever being late on rent for the spacious room she rented in
Queens. Unlike the other operators, even Amparo, she didn't
have to send money back to her home country to add a second
story to the family home. She didn't have to support twins or
parents with a long list of medications either. Aside from the
rent Josefina Lacouture charged her for that spacious room,
her paycheck was all hers. Around three hundred dollars. She
could get front row tickets for a concert at Madison Square
Garden or buy bathing suits at the 34th Street Macy's. It was
even enough for an Oscar de la Renta miniskirt that Josefina
sold her for a third of the original price. Her landlady worked
in Manhattan in the workshop of the famous designer, who

wouldn't hesitate to discard garments for minor imperfections, one sleeve half an inch shorter than the other or a double stitch on an inside hem.

Excited about the renewal of her contract at the lab, she donned her gloves and started to cut a new roll of slides. She inserted the strip, looked through the machine's viewfinder, and moved the first photo into view. At first, she didn't understand. A forest, a pink blur, some red eyes looking at the camera, an animal's smooth back. She still didn't understand the composition but cut and moved quickly onto the next slide. A stable appeared in the viewfinder, two women squatting, and a dun horse. This time it took her a couple seconds. Ignoring the other figures, she focused on the animal's snout. It's nostrils were flared and its neck glistened, maybe it'd been galloping and the sweat had given it that sheen. She turned her attention to the other side of the image and saw the hand of one of the women. It was gripping a dark rod that stuck out between the horse's hindlegs. Yes, a rod, a piece of wood. That's what she wanted to believe, that was her naïve way of protecting herself. Her saliva thickened like petroleum, and she had to stop the machine. She could hear her own breathing, heavy, uneven. She looked at the other operators. Amparo, in the corner, repositioning the cardboard frames into which the cut slides fit. Loretta, quietly singing the same song as always, something about a river shining by the light of the moon. Those two and all the rest, close to a hundred operators, continued on unaware that, for Gloria, barely twenty years old, the world had suddenly assumed the weight of lead and the putrid odor of a tannery. One more, to understand, to be sure. She looked through the viewfinder again and moved on to the next slide, she remembers now in La Mallorquina, smoking a freshly lit and trembling cigarette. This time, it wasn't hard to compose the scene, in a way, her eyes were prepared, she was expecting it. A smiling woman, naked. A German shepherd wearing a muzzle. A bathtub. And then there were more photographs, but by that time she'd already recoiled from the viewfinder. When she failed to step on the pedal to stop it, the machine began spitting out slides cut in half. They fell to the floor and her coworkers turned to look with terror. Miscutting one photograph meant getting chewed out by management; miscutting a whole strip, the possibility of being tossed out into the street without a second thought. Someone, she doesn't know who, came over and quickly turned off the machine. The women's deranged smile clung to her hands, to the nape of her neck, to her spine. In a daze she walked to the bathroom. She didn't throw up the tuna sandwich, just thick saliva. She knelt in front of the toilet bowl until Amparo knocked on the door. Gloria, Glorita. She took a deep breath and told her what she could while splashing water on her face. When she got back to the cutting room, Mr. Murray was standing there, looking at the photographs that hadn't been cut in half. He made a stack of them and, along with the scraps of celluloid, put them inside one of those long, transparent boxes, similar to a soap dish, that they gave all the customers. Before walking away, he looked at her and, in a soft whisper, said: I'm so sorry. She believed him, Mr. Murray was a decent man. He gave her the afternoon off. She walked down Roosevelt Avenue more slowly than usual, half in a trance, half-drunk without having had a drink. She skipped her afternoon English class and didn't even look in the shop window of the Jewish bakery where she always bought an apple strudel. When she got home, she still had no appetite. She told Josefina she wasn't feeling well. Nothing serious, most likely just a cold. Take a Mejoral. Okay, yes, thank you. She put the pill in a drawer, shut herself in her room, and lay there, staring up at the ceiling. When her landlady told her Tigre was on the phone, she said she couldn't talk now. In bed, almost mummified, she felt as if all the energy had been sucked out of her with a huge syringe. Night fell and she feared she would have nightmares about the women, especially that smile. But she didn't dream about anything disturbing and in the morning woke up feeling light and hungry. She was looking at herself in the mirror and brushing her hair, getting ready to go to the lab, when she remembered everything that had happened and the carousel of those images began turning again, indefatigable, magnetic, deafening. Who took the pictures? Who was behind the camera? That day, at work, her coworkers told her over lunch break that the year before, another operator had gotten a roll of a man who'd blown his head off. His brains had been sprayed across the dining room, right in front of an empty highchair. She imagined the baby she used to take care of staring up at her from his cradle.

For several days, whenever she inserted a new roll into the machine, she felt a vague nausea, the blood pounding through her veins, sand on her palate, but then the hours ended up doing what they always do. Time, that great wire brush, filing down the edges first and then scratching the day out of her memory, giving her life back to her. Until she heard those words: Guess what? They came for the pictures.

"C'mon, let's go, Gloria Lucía, we're late."

Gloria Lucía. That's what he calls her when he's trying to seem serious or offended. She checks the time again before looking at him: 4:58 p.m. No, no, no, Tigre, there's no time to fight. She leaves money on the table, picks up the pack of cigarettes and her purse, where she stashed a camera and a silk patterned headscarf to tie around her neck in case it's cool when the concert is over. A little girl approaches the old man who kept her company all afternoon and helps him to his feet while Tigre grabs the mallorca, takes a big bite, and sets it back down on the plate without a shred of guilt. Immediately, they're moving, Tigre and she, a pair of firefighters springing into action.

They walk hurriedly toward the Jackson Heights station. At some point, maybe in front of the only Colombian restaurant in the area, where one time they drank glasses of aguardiente and danced boleros, but not too close, because they were just starting to date, Tigre begins pulling her and she has to let go and stop for a second to keep from falling on her face. It's not easy to walk quickly in the platforms she's wearing. He stops too. He understands and waits. They don't look at each other, neither wanting to trigger a fight. Gloria takes a deep breath, no more apple strudel, she tells herself and starts walking but doesn't take his hand again. They should've asked to borrow the van. Some Latino station is definitely playing some of his songs ahead of the concert. They would've been driving with the radio on and she would be happily singing along instead of feeling this anxiety in her chest. That morning, as she was picking out her earrings, a pair of huge red hoops, she turned on the radio that Josefina had given her and by pure chance happened to hear him being interviewed live from his room at the American Hotel, on Seventh Avenue between 52nd and 53rd. She's walked past that hotel before. The tallest hotel in the world, they say. Two thousand rooms, and he was staying in one of them. He slept and showered in one of them. Him. A few weeks before, he'd been awarded three gold records and one platinum record by his label for his album sales, the interviewer reminded everyone before moving on to questions. Four million, two hundred and fifty thousand records, including the one she purchased in Bogotá and locked away in her bedroom. She listened carefully, getting used to the weight of her earrings, even though she knew pretty well what he would say. She had heard him interviewed so many times that she could predict his answers. How does it make you feel to know that tonight you're going to play Madison Square Garden, at almost the exact time that Apollo 13 will be launched into space? That was the last question. There was a long silence followed by a throat clearing, the sound of a lighter. With his beautiful unapologetic smoker's voice he said: This is where words die. She had to sit down on her bed to comprehend the magnitude of that sentence. This-is-where-words-die. Her eyes teared up as she repeated it in a whisper.

The van. Why doesn't Carlos Arturo ever want to let them use it, she wonders, taking big strides along the sidewalk. Tigre has proposed to his cousin several times that he stay in the office and take care of the paperwork at the agency, but Carlos Arturo would sooner hyperventilate than let

Tigre drive. After returning from Vietnam, where he served one long year, Carlos Arturo spent several months drifting around Queens. Poor guy, he was wandering the streets, was the expression Tigre used, as they walked through Flushing Meadows. Tigre was the one, having just arrived from Colombia, who came up with the idea for the business. He spent weeks working on the project until he got everything arranged and finally sold his cousin on the idea. He made it all so straightforward that Carlos Arturo had no choice but to accept. With a portion of his veteran's pension, they purchased the white van, a desk at a location on the edge of Corona, which they share with a one-armed Puerto Rican lawyer, and had flyers printed. Pretty soon they'd stitched together a wide network of possible customers, starting with Colombians and then branching out to all Spanish-speakers who were interested in specialized tours. The whole thing ran with the precision of a new toaster, and they hardly had any days off. First were the outings to the Statue of Liberty, to Governors Island, to the beaches in Elizabeth, New Jersey, then to more remote destinations like Niagara Falls. Running the agency, Carlos Arturo suffered fewer episodes, though sometimes he still made dark comments. He let one slip at a birthday party they'd all attended recently. The startling impression made by his macabre words remained very present in her mind: I would trade all these fuckers for just one of the men I saw die over there, he said, pointing with his mouth at the couples dancing and sipping piña coladas, made with a bottle of Tres Esquinas someone had brought from Colombia. She knew from Tigre that, in Vietnam, he'd been a member of the tunnel rats, which is what they called soldiers responsible for going into the Vietcong tunnels and blowing them up, soldiers generally of very short stature. Carlos Arturo was barely five feet two. For that reason, he had a deep fear of nature, of everything about it, not just of snakes, spiders, and scorpions, the creatures that he'd encountered more than once in those tunnels. He was one of the few people in the city unmoved by the transformation of the trees with the arrival of spring, or by the reflection of the sun on the Hudson. My thing is the concrete, the buildings, the bodegas. The trash in the streets!, he said with a crooked smile that cut across his face like a knife wound. He'd left Colombia with his parents when he was twelve years old and had never gone back. That country is pure forest, even the cities look like forests. There aren't any true cities there, not like this, they all seem on the brink of collapse, he said whenever their homeland came up. It all sounded like a joke, like a schtick, but sometimes it scared Tigre. A couple months ago, his cousin told him he was going to sleep in the van so he could always be on the street. Tigre responded with that scowl he deploys when he's being impossible. It appears on his face only on occasion, a thunderbolt. She's one of the few people who doesn't fear it.

At last, they're just steps away from the glowing entrance of the subway station. They go up the stairs and at the turnstiles insert one of those strange coins that I would find many years later in a drawer, rummaging around for hours to ward off the boredom of vacation afternoons, a coin that wasn't big and was lighter than any I'd held before. It was stamped with NYC. The Y was actually a slot. One night, when she arrived home from the office enveloped in her typical blend of smog and Opium by Yves Saint Laurent, the perfume she wore for years, I showed her the coin and asked: What can you buy with this? She might have scolded me for having gone through her things. But no reprimand came. Seeing it, her eyes sparkled, she took the little piece of metal and held it in her open palm as if it were a baby bird. It's a token. For the subway, I heard her say, and it might have been right then, in that moment, that I started writing all of this that I'm writing now. Seeing my disconcerted face, she explained: the New York metro . . . a train that travels throughout the city underground. I imagined a metal serpent devouring mountains of earth and stone. It frightened me. And her? For those few seconds, she vanished, she was no longer there with me, in that house in Bogotá, contending with the indiscretions of her husband, who from one day to the next joined the Sharks Swimming Club and began to go to the pool two or three nights a week. Swimming, the perfect excuse to be gone for a few hours and to come home freshly showered. For a few seconds, she ceased to be the secretary of the customs director, frightened by all the strange things that were happening in her office, briefcases full of cash passed between bathroom stalls, and in the blink of an eye she was once again standing in front of a subway station, the same station where now it finally dawns on her what Tigre is wearing. She admires his tight pants, the bottle-green shirt, the boots, the belt that she gave him for his birthday. Like her, he's dressed for a party. There's no debate, he's officially handsome and she loves how he dresses, just the opposite of the Cuban teacher from the language academy she went out with for a few days. It ended when the imbecile tried to forcibly kiss her in a movie theater. A picture, yes. She opens her purse, takes out her camera, and calls to him. Tigre!, she raises her voice, Tigreee!! He turns around with a start, but when he sees her focusing on him, he breaks into a full smile. He's not one of those men you have to beg for a smile. It still surprised her, all those teeth. Click. Done. Divine. For a second, she thinks about who might develop the photograph. She's going to send the roll to Agfa. What if she got to cut it? It would be the perfect spell to distance her from those other photos. Or at least let it be Amparo who gets to do it. In the distance she hears the purring of the subway. Let's go, it's coming!, she hears him say. She puts the camera in her purse, missing the train at that point would mean missing the concert, she bounds up the remaining stairs two at a time, dodging the people coming down, office workers, women with children, a musician, two rabbis, and lets Tigre take her by the hand so that now, yes, he can pull her along a little, the final stretch. They make it inside the third car just as the doors close. They laugh and embrace for a long time, as if they still can't believe that it's going to be a great night.

After a few stops, they find open seats. For a few minutes, they don't say anything, she just rests her head on his shoulder. She feels his breathing, smells the snowy pine forest of his cologne. She closes her eyes, hoping to fall asleep, but, frustrated, quickly abandons the idea the way one abandons a fountain pen that's run out of ink. She pulls her head away from his shoulder and turns her face forty-five degrees toward him.

"If you could talk to your mom now, what would you ask her?"

Tigre's mother died in a landslide when he was seven. A rock flattened the car she was traveling in. It happened at night and they never found her body. Their mutual orphanhood, tragic, confessed at Caesar's, the Times Square restaurant where, according to him, they sell the best french fries in the city, the place he took her on their first date, skipped them three or four spaces ahead in the conquest game.

"Wait, what?"

"What would you ask your mother if you could talk to her now?"

"I don't get it. How do you mean? You mean if she hadn't died? If she were alive?" Tigre brushed back the hair that had fallen across his forehead.

"No, no. If she could answer you from the afterlife. What would you ask her?"

"The afterlife . . . the afterlife. The dead don't have mouths, Gloria Lucía."

"I know, Tigre . . . but if they did, if they could speak, what would you ask her?"

"Ah, it's a game, I see. Okay." This puts Tigre in a good mood. He likes games. Or better, bets. "Well, let's see, I would ask her if she's been alone all this time."

"Umm, good question. I always imagined them together, I mean, people who knew each other when they were alive, like in a big movie theater that's slowly filling up. But maybe they're all alone. Each of them, alone. The whole world for each of them, and all of them wandering through it. But that would be hell, right? A world just like this one, identical, but alone. The streets vacant, this subway."

"I guess. What about you? What would you ask your father?"

Gloria takes a minute to think. The question wasn't a game for her. Tomorrow, if Amparo can pull it off, she will talk to her father. It occurs to her that she could bring rice and make him a nice bowl. Her father had loved freshly cooked rice, according to her mother. Sometimes that was all he ate, a big, fragrant bowl, still steaming.

"Where do they sell the best rice in Queens? Uncooked, I mean."

Tigre turns to look at her, overreacting. Gloria smiles with her green eyes, wanting to erase the question. The car doors open, distracting them for a second. It's the last stop before crossing the river, and the train almost always fills up. Gloria watches the crowd as it presses in to see if she can pick out somebody interesting; when no one draws her attention, she has no choice but to face Tigre, to confront the awkwardness that always arises whenever she trails off or unexpectedly diverts their conversations, like someone swerving in the middle of the road to miss an animal or an apparition. But then she recognizes Raúl next to a window. He's alone, without Mary, blue tie, white shirt, shiny shoes. He must be going to the store to lock the register. She cranes her neck a little to see him better through the crowd. It would be pointless to try to catch his attention by waving, he's pretty far away.

Tigre senses her giraffe-like movement and looks in the same direction. He sees Raúl too. He says nothing. Stony silence is the weapon Tigre tends to deploy when he disapproves of something. He's conceited, is the only thing he's been able to articulate to justify his animosity toward her landlady's son. Disappointed by the unconsummated greeting, Gloria swerves again to correct the direction of the conversation. She restarts it the easiest way possible, a lie:

"I want to make beans and invite everyone over, but I don't think the rice that Josefina buys is very good."

Ah, I see, makes sense, you're not losing your mind, Tigre appears to tell himself, offering an informed response:

"Yeah. People say that the Indian place sells delicious rice." After a short pause, he adds: "But I really doubt it." Tigre is a little racist in his own way. He conceals it by discrediting others.

"At the Indian shop? See? I had no idea. I'll check it out."

"So. What would you ask him?"

"Who?"

Frustrated at not being able to build a conversation pillar by pillar, Tigre raises his voice:

"Your father!"

Someone in the corner turns to look. Everyone else has long grown accustomed to sudden shouts on the subway.

"Hey, no need to shout. Let's see. Um, I would ask him..."

Gloria concentrates like when doing writing exercises at boarding school. She thought she could write them without moving her hand, with just the power of her mind. Think, she says to herself, think, think, but a few seconds later she realizes she doesn't have a clue what she would ask him. When she made the appointment with Amparo, she thought she would have thousands of questions, a job interview to rehire him, to let him back into her life after a seventeen-year absence. Tigre doesn't press her, but he doesn't let it go either.

"You never told me how they killed him. I just know he was shot."

"A shot to the heart," Gloria specifies, emphasizing the final word, her hand gliding with the smoothness of a paper airplane, touching down briefly on her chest.

It's true, she hasn't wanted to tell him. She hasn't wanted to tell him that her thirty-six-year-old father had been with a friend at one of his farms, paying his workers, and that, at nightfall, instead of going by his office to organize the pages of a lawsuit, he went to drink a double aguardiente at the Ambos Mundos Café. She hasn't wanted to tell him that the brother of the owner, a man born in Colón shortly after the separation of Panama, liberal down to his bunions, came in wasted, ordered an aguardiente as well, and from an adjoining table sat listening to the conversation between her father and his friend. They always talked politics, not for nothing was he the only child of the conservative leader in the area, and when he sat down on a bench with the party director, everyone had to vacate the town plaza. What they said must've upset the Panamanian, causing him walk over to their table and whisper something in her father's ear. No one ever knew what he said, but whatever it was, it made her father leap to his feet and challenge the man to a duel. They went out to the corner with their weapons because, of course, both were armed, this was the fifties and the fire started on April 9 by the assassination of the man who would've become president was burning more fiercely than ever in their province, conservatives versus liberals, blues versus reds. The incredible thing was that the last case her father had taken before the Panamanian put a bullet in his chest under the shade of a rain tree had him defending the liberal-led railroad union of Armenia, a city located in the western foothills of the Andes, in a dispute with the state company. He'd decided to take the case *pro bono*. That was the kind of lawyer he was, contradictory, generous, blue and red. And she hadn't wanted to tell Tigre that some of her father's friends had picked him up off the ground, his shirt soaked in blood, and brought him home, where his wife was waiting to have dinner with him and their daughters. She was the youngest of the three. They killed Mendoza! They killed Mendoza!, rang out in the streets until midnight. People said he would have been the next governor. And she really didn't want to tell him that there was another version of events that circulated among some members of her family: allegedly, weeks before, her father had shot one of the Panamanian's brothers. And what if he asked her that? If her father's death had actually been an act of revenge?

"And?"

"That's it. A shot to the heart."

"I don't get why the hell I always tell you complete stories and you just give me little pieces. It's crazy."

Tigre says something else, but Gloria doesn't hear it. Instead, she watches Raúl move with a dozen other passengers toward the doors of the subway car. They've arrived at the 53rd Street station, which means they're getting close. Then, surprisingly, Tigre falls silent. He stops complaining, unusual for him. Following his line of sight, she sees a well-dressed man slipping his hand into a woman's purse. Tigre stiffens and is about to shout something to prevent the theft. She squeezes his hand as hard as she can. If there's a fight, they won't get to the concert on time. Tigre furiously shakes free of her hand and looks away. Gloria watches as the man moves toward the door with the woman's wallet in his pocket. Before exiting, the thief turns and gives her a brief, mocking glance. The doors close and the train pulls out for Times Square. Instead of being scandalized, she's impressed by the pickpocket's meticulous elegance.

"And what if he'd robbed that idiot, Raúl? Would we have said nothing then too?" she hears Tigre say.

The camera. She wants to make sure she still has it, that someone hasn't gotten a hand in her purse. She opens it fearfully, but there it is, the Kodak Instamatic X-15, super light and practically unbreakable, which she's used to take pictures of the city since she arrived. She reviews the counter without removing it from her purse. Perfect, fifteen left on the roll. She'll probably take ten at the concert and have five left for after. It was actually Raúl who went with her to buy it. They met at his pipe-and-tobacco shop just off Central Park, red doormat, wood-framed display cases, the smell of rolling tobacco. That's why Tigre looks down on him, because Raúl is everything he's not.

Supposedly, Carlota and Torero would be waiting for them at the entrance to the Felt Forum at Madison Square Garden. The nickname, Torero, meaning the bullfighter, unlike Tigre, functioned by opposition: the Uruguayan is afraid of blood. The two men watch each other's back without ever having gotten that close; the important thing is that it's clear to them that they need each other. On the two occasions that the four of them have gone out together, the women dominated the conversation and the men, so focused on their drinks, only interjected with an occasional laugh or superficial remark. There's something about the two women that, when they're together, drains everyone else. They're energy extractors, human magnets, a brutal force nourished by nighttime secrets shared under the roof of Gloria's landlady and Carlota's mother, Josefina.

Emerging at the corner of 33rd Street and Eighth Avenue, she sees the line, a thread of ants winding around the block. Gloria and Tigre move along it, searching for their friends, afraid they've already gone in. They spot them up ahead, mere yards from the doors. Gloria counts three fire trucks and three ambulances outside the stadium. A cadre of policemen with nightsticks quickens her pulse. The handshake between Tigre and Torero is but a transaction compared to Carlota's embrace, kiss, and hand on Gloria's shoulder, affirming her existence, a way of saying, you've come this far, well done. They don't ask why they're late, and Tigre and Gloria don't offer an explanation. They've all made a silent pact, ensuring that from now on nothing can go wrong. The line starts to move. There are murmurs, here or there a flinch-inducing shriek. Carlota, the most careful of the four, extracts the tickets from her purse and ceremoniously distributes them, consecrated communion. Some of the men can't help but stare at her, tall and tan, with long black hair spilling heavily down her back like an exotic plant, another bodily organ to admire.

Torero has been in love with her for three weeks, or, at the very least, he hasn't been able to stop thinking about her while working for his family's moving company or practicing with his band. That's why Carlota is dating him, because he's in a band. What a strange thing it is to think of someone, to have their image occupy first a few seconds, then a few minutes, and finally multiple hours a day, even conquering your dreams, to have them spread like a drop of ink in water, first to your stomach, then to your lungs, then to your throat, until they occupy even your nasal cavities and behind your eyes, until they fill your entire skull. That's what Torero feels, a possession. An intoxication.

Moving slowly forward, tickets in hand, they pass the turnstiles, cross the lobby, and make their way through the bodies, overheated with waiting. Some arrived at midday, with the sun at its zenith, and a handful slept in front of the auditorium door. Their boyfriends' bodies serve as attacking tanks. All they have to do is slip through behind them, with false smiles, bumping shoulders, excusing themselves here and there. Once they've reached a good spot, Gloria relaxes and slowly takes in her surroundings, she wants to acknowledge the terrain, like one of those astronauts scheduled soon to land on the moon. There are thousands of fifteen-year-olds with their mothers, hundreds of couples their same age, and others who are two or three times as old. Nearby someone has a small radio tuned to the same station she was listening to that morning. She recognizes the reporter's voice, he's describing some of the singer's activities, he reports that during rehearsal he smoked three packs of Kents. Two cigarettes per song. The radio commentary blends in with the cadences of Spanish from all corners of Latin America. No country has been left out of sending its troops to see the King. Their King, not the King of the gringos, so tailor-made for them. Gloria has never gone to a concert and much less to one like the one that's about the start. She's only ever attended dances with big orchestras, the Noche de San Silvestre in 1966 or the day her twin sisters were presented in society at the Club América in her city, which in reality is a large town that decades ago got rich off the coffee bonanza, which her family figured out how to benefit from in different ways, only to subsequently lose half of what they'd made. Other than that, she's gone to parties in Palermo, in her neighborhood, at the Viejo Caldas Student Housing, or spent time dancing with friends in the main hall of her house. Only after, of course, gathering the china and rolling up the rugs, you're not going to get them covered with ash, she heard her mother proclaim from her throne. This is very different, in part precisely because she's beyond her mother's reach and because of the crowd that, instead of overwhelming, embraces her. She feels accompanied and certain that she hasn't blown any of this out of proportion.

Everyone around her must have a similar story. Hers includes hundreds of oatmeal cookies baked every Saturday afternoon of the year she discovered, in the full bloom of adolescence, his voice, that voice, while her sisters entertained their suitors. Instead of bringing the cookies into the visiting room to share with everyone, Gloria ate them alone in her bedroom, slowly, one by one, staring at his album covers, enraptured, listening to him sing. Side A, side B. Side B, side A. And now, now she was going to see him live.

"We're going to see him! Live!" Carlota whispered in her ear, reading her mind, and to allow them to relish the thrill, to hold on to that moment, I think about a night of my own, spent not far from where they are now.

It's also a Saturday, also spring, 1998, powerful waves of static electricity shake the streets and I'm there, in New York, because of her and her golden subway token, the metal serpent that more than devouring earth and stones has devoured great chunks of time, uniting our ways of being young. That day, one of the waitresses from the café where I worked for six months washing dishes invited me to the Bank. On Saturdays, they do "Albion Nights" and you have to dress accordingly, Nikolett Balogh, Nikki, the Hungarian fashion-design student, explained. We met at the exit to the subway. I wasn't particularly dressed up, just wearing black, whereas she had rented a wedding dress and had makeup on that made her look even paler than she was. Seeing me in the light of a streetlamp, she removed an eyeliner from her small purse, took me by the chin, and carefully, with great concentration, made up my eyes. I felt her fruity breath on my face. Before crossing over to the corner of East Houston and Essex where the club was located, a young man appeared beside me, dressed head to toe in black velvet, a bow tie, long, undulating hair, and a monocle. It took me a minute to recognize what was sitting on his shoulder: a desiccated crow. We stood for a long minute at the intersection, but I couldn't stop looking at the animal out of the corner of my eye in shock. Among Báthory countesses and Victorian couples, we lined up at the entrance to the club, which occupied an old bank. Once inside, the Hungarian led me by the hand to the enormous bar on the second floor and we ordered the first of several vodka cranberries that we would drink that night. We toasted, once, twice, three times, we talked about our boss, she waved to some acquaintances, who soon surrounded her, and at some point I left her behind, to circulate through the bar. I did one lap and ended up leaning on a handrail. From my position, I saw a cage hanging from the ceiling with a half-naked woman dancing inside, and beyond, a man in the crowd sitting on a stool and drawing men and women made up identically to the people in the posters I had on the walls of my room as a teenager in the mountains of a devastated city, and, way in the back, the young man dressed in velvet. I went down the stairs, crossed the dance floor, and stopped about a yard away from him, drink in hand, and watched him whisper things to his crow and pause theatrically to hear its response, and I waited too, listening, expectant. Albion. Nikki found me after a while and dragged me, somewhat drunk, out onto the dance floor. The song playing made her euphoric and there we were, jumping and dancing, in each other's arms in a legendary bar at the end of the twentieth century, on a night that's nothing but the prolongation of the night Gloria is about to have. The two of us, in New York, at exactly the same age: twenty years old.

Carlotaaaa! Someone is shouting louder and louder from somewhere. Carlotaaaa! Finally they locate the source, it's coming from the box seats next to the stage. It's Tito, a Dominican who also works in Oscar de la Renta's workshop. Carlota turns and tells her at a thousand miles an hour that the designer wanted to meet the singer and got the manager to let him go backstage before the show to visit him and Tito had found out and asked if he could go along. And the designer said yes! Carlota finished and looked back at the box seats. He's a survivor; she waves both hands at Tito and his smile, which doesn't square with anything her friend had told her while they watched the news with TV dinner trays atop their legs. A few months before, Tito had been in Greenwich

Village with a friend at a place where men dress as women and women as men, Carlota explained. That day, Tito's friend was wearing a long dress, makeup, and a wig. At midnight, the raid came, they shut off the music, lined up the attendants, and searched them. They separated the ones wearing dresses. They dragged all of them out into the street, tore off their wigs. People from the neighborhood began to gather around. Vans came to take them away and a policeman started shoving Tito's friend. The Dominican intervened. Another policeman struck him on the back of the legs and then on the forehead. A rush of blood, a commotion, stones and coins raining down from all directions, and Tito didn't know who pulled him out of there with his shirt soaking wet. They took his friend to a station, where he spent the whole night in lockup. They spat on him multiple times. Tito was left with a scar over his right eye and a shudder every time he saw a policeman in the street. After that day, he stopped going to bars and sometimes wept with rage alone in the workshop. Josefina had witnessed it and had consoled him. He was shaking, the poor man, Carlota says her mother said, but today he's beaming, because he's there to see the singer perform.

Carlota leaves her to go over to Tito, who is still calling to her insistently. Maybe they'll let her go backstage too. If that happens, the night will be complete. Gloria doesn't feel envious, she's never let that feeling—to her mind, the vilest of all—take root. Look, he's coming out, someone shouts and points insistently at one corner. So distracted, she suddenly remembers the camera in her purse that she hasn't gotten ready for his appearance. She takes it out carefully, puts on the flash, which looks like an ice cube, and focuses on the stage. As soon as he emerges, she'll be ready to take three to five shots and then enjoy herself, she's not going to spend the concert with the device in her hand, but before the lights come down, someone bumps her hard and the camera falls out of her hands. She feels her right thigh help to break its fall, then how it ricochets off her calf and is lost, deep in the void. She ducks down. In the darkness, she glimpses a forest of legs, swaying reeds. Thanks to a spotlight that swings by overhead and filters down to the floor, she locates the camera nearby, next to a pair of horrendous white shoes. It'll take her two seconds to reach it and one more to bend down. Her plan, if anguish and desperation can be called a plan, is foiled before it can be put into action. Someone kicks the camera and sends it flying as the murmur, a buzzing of hornets, swells and multiplies and is soon replaced by hysterical shrieks. She starts to feel short of breath. She lifts her head, finds Tigre, tries to tell him what happened, shouts at him, gestures with her hands, maybe he can push his way through and grab her camera. He should, then she would forgive him for making her wait. Her stupidity quickly dawns on her, it would be like asking him to stand in front of an avalanche. Nothing, it's okay, don't worry, and Tigre nods, nothing, nothing, but she's lost her camera, her camera, the first thing she bought when she got to New York, and a sorrow like the kind that'll fall from the heavens like an anvil when the world ends envelops her from head to toe.

An announcer in a red-wine bow tie speaks to the buzzing crowd, and try as she might, she can't understand what he says. Not a word. She wants to cry. For a second, she says she doesn't want to be there anymore, which is like saying she doesn't want to be alive. She doesn't want to wait for Tigre at some diner anymore, she doesn't want to think about her murdered father anymore, she doesn't want to feel guilty for having more money in her wallet than Amparo anymore, she doesn't want to have the image of the dog in the bathtub, his protruding tongue, the naked woman touching him, in her head anymore. She has an urge to rend the flesh off someone's face, to kick the forest of legs she glimpsed a few seconds before, to howl at her mother and ask her why she never loved her. Carlota comes back just in time and puts an arm around her. Carlota understands. Carlota is a true friend in that city where many, thousands, don't have a single friend. She tries to kiss her cheek, but it lands on her mouth because of shoving in the crowd and they laugh. She begs her to repeat the first things the announcer said. She thought she heard sixteen countries, two hundred fifty million, something like that. *The first concert via satellite from Madison Square Garden. The only Latin American who has ever performed on this grand stage*, she answers, very serious, holding her face with both hands, staring at her with dilated pupils, bottomless pools, black olives. The only one, Gloria repeats. The announcer slips away, a heavy curtain rises, and the orchestra appears. Maybe they're the same musicians she saw on El Show de las Estrellas last year, with her sisters, in front of the television. Could they be? Because she's thinking about this, she doesn't see him emerge from the right corner of the stage. Carlota's long, enameled fingernails digging into her forearm alerts her. He's already center stage by the time she focuses on him. He's wearing a violet jacket, orange shirt, black pants, black boots, and probably red socks. She's heard that he uses them to frighten away envy. His head seems a little too big, but there's no doubt that it's him. Him. Him. Him. His tousled head of hair, his long sideburns, his chest adorned with that heavy gold medallion. And his smile. And his eyes, with which he seems to look one by one, face by face, at the thousands who have come to worship him. From here, from my position in the shadows, I force the King to pause for a few extra seconds on Gloria, to make her feel his power in her knees, which shake uncontrollably. And following that long look, the great Sandro, Sandro de América, Sandro el

Gitano, wraps the microphone cord around his hand a couple of times and turns it into a whip. Then his forehead tilts to the heavens and in a few seconds the agonizing weeks of waiting for that voice of voices are left behind, a flood of golden light bathes everything.

The concert lasts almost two hours. It's a confused mix of religious ecstasy, running mascara, thighs rubbing against each other, hot sweat, and sensual howls. At a certain point, the abandon is such that the police have to come in and impose order in the front rows. Several women attempt to climb onstage and some even faint. The singer jokes after the five-minute intermission that he uses to change clothes. He deploys the microphone against the palm of his hand like a judge's gavel to demand: Order! Order in the court! Gloria has never gotten drunk, she's been tipsy, sure, but drunk, never. She assumes it must be something like what she ends up experiencing at the concert. She doesn't know how she made it to the end, how she's still standing, but she is, and Sandro, now in a white smoking jacket, pink shirt, and white boots, is getting ready for his final number, the farewell that nobody wants. He demands complete silence. Guided by a barely perceptible drumroll and by the star's gesticulations, the tamed audience feels the electricity ascend from the tips of their boots, pass through their groins, and continue into their stomachs. The flow is cut off by the inevitable whispers.

He scolds the audience, with true outrage, a dictator threatening to never again return to that balcony, to never let himself be seen again until he's embalmed. He's called for complete silence, and he'll go to his dressing room if his command isn't obeyed. He begins the ritual again and now the electric current can rise free of obstacles to the chest and neck. When the vibration reaches the tip of his tongue, the longed-for "Rosa, Rosa" issues forth. The name hangs in the air of Madison Square Garden until, little by little, its letters open up. Out of nowhere, she has an urge to look at Tigre. She turns and doesn't find him beside her. Another man has taken his place, his warmth is different, greasy. She's lost him, she doesn't know when, or how. She looks at the faces around her and, on the brink of panic, locates him up in front of her, pressed against the stage, surrounded by women with half-open blouses. She's no longer that interested in Sandro and his farewell, she doesn't know why. She's more focused on her boyfriend, who contorts as if possessed until, a second before the song ends, she sees him cry out with euphoria. *Rosa, Rosa, tan maravillosa como blanca diosa.* The same Tigre who obliges her to always be checking her watch, the sometimes elusive and inconsiderate Tigre, of sudden and devastating silences, that Tigre now weeps uncontrollably, finally opened up to a world where all worlds fit, including hers, and Gloria feels something she's never felt before: she feels, tingling on the tip of her tongue, the taste of intoxication. The tears streaming down his face make her think of the future.

Not far from the exit to the Felt Forum, the remnants of the collective hypnosis are still perceptible in the shining eyes of some concertgoers, in their childish excitement, in their comments, did you see when he threw himself on the ground and rolled around?, and what about when he put that flower in his mouth?, and the woman who jumped on him?, good thing the police grabbed her. For her part, Gloria believes she's left the experience, the event, behind, contrary to what yesterday she would've sworn would happen, those hours of frenzied excitement anticipated yesterday, staring at the ceiling, hands crossed over her belly while Carlota slept in her bed, sideways. The concert is part of the past, she tells herself, certain, and that certainty makes her feel a kind of superiority to the others now dispersing into the night, Tito and his friend among them. Carlota greets him, happy but drained. Gloria, in better shape, though barely, wonders if this is the friend who dresses as a woman. His eyebrows are striking, meticulously waxed, from what she can see.

"He was lovely. The boss gave him a shirt and he tried it on in front of us. You can't imagine."

"He took his clothes off in front of you? You saw him naked?" Carlota asks.

"Yes!"

The man's mannerisms make Tigre and Torero uncomfortable, their nicknames weighing them down like stones around their necks.

"Waist up," Tito's friend clarifies, tersely.

The discomfort compounds the expansive fatigue left by adrenaline withdrawing like a low tide. Tito, reading his friend, who clearly doesn't want to spend a single second with those two men, gets ahead of any intention of going out to celebrate the concert together.

"Sorry, we have a commitment," Tito says.

"We're organizing a march," his companion points out.

Tito elbows him, eliminating the possibility of an explanation.

"Adiós, chicas. Say hi to your mom. Nice to meet you, boys," he says without addressing Torero or Tigre directly. They move off silently, floating, and leave the four of them there, fixed to the pavement.

Tigre is the first to react. He suggests they walk down Seventh Avenue to Times Square and catch the subway from there back to Queens. It's a pleasant night, so nobody argues, despite how their heels and knees ache from so much standing.

Quickly, Gloria and Tigre get ahead of the other two. Alone, with the most cautious voice she's capable of, she brings up the end of the concert, the passion of his tears. She expected denial, but not for it to be so emphatic. So forceful. I didn't cry—that's bullshit. But it doesn't matter what he says or how he says it. She knows what she saw and that's enough for her to believe in what the future might bring. Even though they've been dating for a couple months, it's only in the last fifty minutes that she's felt it in her bones. Or that's what she tells herself, maybe because she thinks that she'll never see another man cry like that, disconsolate, beautiful in his vulnerability. But she's wrong. She will see another man cry, twenty-three years later in a Miami hotel, but it won't be about the blossoming of love, just the opposite, it'll be about the beginning of the end.

IT'S JANUARY 1983, AND IN ADDITION TO BEING MAR-
ried, they've brought two children, my brother and me, into
their lives. The wind brings in the scent of the sea, a few
blocks away. Yesterday, before the rum-raisin ice cream, we
went to the beach. It was almost empty, the sky was over-
cast, and a few big drops of rain even fell, the kind that seem
pregnant, water inside water. It was just what we needed, to
stretch out on the sand, nothing more. We've dragged our
feet through amusement parks for the last ten days. I was six
years old and was trying out a toy camera that also turned
into a pistol; my brother, three, played with a handful of little
seashells and a stuffed orca. Neither of our parents went in
the water, it was too choppy.

He's stayed behind in the hotel room. The ice cream sat
really badly with him. He's had to go to the bathroom multiple times and is feeling weak. She, on the other hand, has
been able to get ready just as she likes. Red coral necklace,
heavy eye shadow, cotton pantsuit with shoulder pads and a

hint of neckline, sunglasses. At Sea World or Circus World, places that don't really speak to her, but that he insisted on recording with the camcorder he bought specifically for the trip, she felt completely horrendous. And nauseated. She even threw up one of those fast and heavy breakfasts, smothered in sauces, downed at top speed on a bench because the House of Horror was about to close and he had to have images for the family album. She takes me by the hand and pushes the stroller with the other. She feels out of reach to me, much farther than her five feet six inches, five-nine in heels. People move out of the way before us, before the triumvirate that we form upon leaving the hotel. At some point, her attention wanders to a record store a few yards ahead. From a pair of speakers, that song plays at full volume, a melody that's played in cafés, in exchange houses, in ticket booths throughout those weeks of travel. The frenetic opening of the song fills her with energy, and she drags us toward the store. Plus, there's the coincidence, that name—her name. She concentrates, trying to understand the lyrics, and the effort pays off . . . *Are the voices in your head calling Gloriaaa . . .* At the door to the store, answering the call, hearing that someone shouts, above all else, for Gloriaaa . . . ready now to go in and ask for the album, I pull her hard in the other direction and, despite her confusion, she doesn't resist. How many times might I have done that, self-centered and rude?, how many times might she have strayed from her path to attend to mine? I pull her toward a car, parked in an alcove, identical in my mind to the compact spaceship I saw at Epcot. She knows I want to touch it. She lets me go. I already know how to read. Po-rs-rs-che, I whisper, hanging between syllables as I trace my index finger across the gleaming logo. Her hand reaches out from behind my head and imitates me, she touches the bas-relief of the shield with her index finger and gets a static shock. She pulls it back with fright when the owner appears and stands on the opposite side. He rummages for the keys in his pockets and looks at her with curiosity, just her, we're outside his field of vision. He's older, handsome, she thinks as the man smiles slightly. She returns his smile, adding a flirtatious twinkle in her eyes, liberated now from her sunglasses, because the light has begun to fade, receding irremediably, leaving us alone in the helplessness of the coming night. *Nice*, she says, just like that, in English with an accent, and the man responds, challenging and inviting, as he inserts the key and unlocks the doors. *Nice?* Me or the car? Gloriaaa . . . All at once it occurs to her to tell him that we're not her kids. It's credible, she's barely over thirty. They're my sister's, I'm taking care of them, she doesn't hesitate, but then she hears a little voice, mama, mama, that word twice repeated without accent dissuades her and sends that man—to whom it might've also occurred to ask her to get in, his sports car has only two doors anyway, to leave us there, in the middle of the street—fleeing. It should be, it should be possible for her to escape this marriage, which little by little had been becoming a second boarding school. The man gets in the Porsche, turns it on, and pulls away without a word. Within a second, he disappears behind a police patrol car that flies by at top speed. Maybe one of the ones that answered the call from the beginning of our trip or the one that'll pull up an hour later at Hotel Monte Carlo.

It all happened so quickly. She had my brother in her arms and one eye on the luggage while he filled out the hotel registry. Lucia, what's . . . ? In a low voice, he asked for addresses, phone numbers, dates of birth, the things he never remembers. He always uses her middle name; he prefers it to Gloria. Nobody else does that. It's his way of boxing her in. The continental breakfast is included, the concierge answers when he finally finishes the form. Where she's standing, she couldn't see me, but she probably sensed my presence, clinging to his left leg. Always still, always silent, maybe that's why she trusted me.

When I was really little, they'd taken me to the office a couple of times, where they lifted me up and left me standing like a trophy on a big wooden desk, among customs import records and brown folders with the Ministry of Finance logo on them. Their coworkers approached and laughed nervously at my stony attitude. They'd lied to everyone in the office about how we ended up here, in Miami. We won the tickets in a raffle, they said. They lied to the director too, when they ran into him in the office parking garage. He required a more detailed explanation. Yes, we bought the ticket after going shopping on Sunday, Disney with the kids, imagine the luck.

The cash for the trip, and for so many things, had, in effect, fallen from the sky, and the explanation was so simple and at the same time so mysterious that it left them perpetually flummoxed, until the last cent disappeared from their accounts, because they were never the kind of people who knew how to invest, how to manage finances, they were only capable of going to an office and working. That's why they never quit their jobs. It was also a source of shame, especially for her, because she associated it with misbegotten funds, even though it wasn't. None of their coworkers knew, and they would've been hard-pressed to believe them anyway. There would've been animosity, or worse, the rumor that one of those infamous bill-stuffed suitcases the big importers dropped off to have a number here or a date there changed on customs records had come in with their name on it. The truth is that, one Sunday, he'd gone to the racetrack, to Hipódromo de los Andes, with a childhood friend and, without having a clue about horses, had won in a single afternoon what he would earn in a lifetime. The triple crown. And if his friend, who was a professional gambler, hadn't ended up in jail with a fraud conviction the next month, it's quite likely that life at the Hipódromo would've swallowed him up and that Miami and the Hotel Monte Carlo would've never appeared on our horizon.

I'm sure that she saw me out of the corner of her eye when I let go of his left leg and moved away, walked just a few yards, and pushed the button as hard as I could. We were in the middle of the city, on Collins Avenue. If a fire spread throughout the hotel, the banks' central offices and the jewelry chains would be engulfed in flames, so the button set off a siren more appropriate for announcing an air raid than a fire. Though that wasn't the worst part, the truly disturbing thing—which they reiterated multiple times—was the calmness with which, at six years old, I'd stepped back from the wall, put my hands in the pockets of my green corduroys, and turned to look at her defiantly. She confessed to me once that during the first days of my life, at the clinic, when she bent down to pick me up, she'd been frightened by my stare from the crib. It was the first time our fears collided, I guess. The siren echoed everywhere and within a few minutes, half a dozen fire trucks and police vehicles surrounded the hotel. Guests began appearing in the lobby, dressed in robes, hair disheveled, some trembling in fear even though there was no sign of smoke anywhere. The alarm stopped. The disdainful looks lasted almost an hour, as long as it took to get everyone's statements. They were added to her discomfort before the concierge and her husband's concentric rage. Over time, those disproportionate eruptions were becoming his only possible routine and nobody, not even him, knew what magma produced them. Did I push the button because I wanted to stop the eruptions or feed them? I don't know. Did he grab me roughly by the arm? Did he slap me? I don't think so, he never went that far. Our first and only foreign trip, a trip that put me and my brother inside the circle at school of those who had traveled abroad, the trip that should've officially consolidated our family's good fortune, kicked off with an alarm that continued to ring in our heads for a long time.

Again, the little voice: Mama, mama. She stands there looking at him, at my brother. He's barely cried once; he's been good all vacation and that's a big deal for her. He was born underweight and he'll struggle to concentrate enough to study throughout high school; he'll love punk, he'll try drugs and have girlfriends before me; he'll be the black sheep. Not forever. When he's grown up, he'll have a fit martial artist's body, which I'll envy, and will get a doctorate in tropical agriculture in another language. Nevertheless, he'll have weak eyes his whole life and she'll never stop secretly blaming herself for things she'd done while pregnant. I shouldn't have eaten pork at that cookout. I shouldn't have played with Anís, the cat that belonged to my mother's housekeeper, Pastora, so much. Time and again she's gone over the months of her pregnancy and landed on those two causes to explain the illness. She hated Doctor Reinoso to the point of incandescent lava tears when he explained to her the extent of the virus at the office of his homeopathic practice, but she kept taking my brother to see him, because the Berlin-educated ophthalmologist was the only one who saw any hope, everyone else had recommended that, when the moment came, she enroll him at a special school. Instead, Reinoso recommended giving him a drink with sago flour, a tuber with powerful curative powers that she'd never heard of before. And that's what she's done, day after day. Just before leaving the hotel, she gave it to him in a baby's bottle. If a life could be contained in a handful of words, her list would always include *Agfa laboratories* and *toxoplasmosis*, maybe the name of the Jewish family she worked for as housekeeper too, but they wouldn't appear until much later.

A year before traveling to Miami, the viral load surpassed the limit set by Doctor Reinoso and they had to take extreme measures. Both of them, because he's been there, with her, it must be said, first running a brush of very fine bristles across her bare back every morning, then putting clay on her chest and two little flakes of gold over her eyes at night. They also started going to the Bojacá church on Sundays. A married couple from the city who travel to a remote village to pray among a crowd of campesinos with ponchos smelling of sheep and rain. In the rectory, she bought a small block of yellow wax with the eyes of Santa Lucía in relief, she had it blessed and stuck it in a drawer, alongside an album commemorating our births. Women the world over keep baby teeth and locks of their children's hair, as if they might one day need them to cast a spell.

We resume our pleasant drifting, ignoring the fact that two minutes ago the owner of a Porsche was on the brink of separating us. How long has she been thinking about that? About leaving? We reenter the flow of the street and let ourselves be swept lazily along for a few blocks until we run aground in front of a huge supermarket. We pass by display racks of frozen food, trays of the TV dinners that she came to know in Queens, that she was able to prepare one day and not the next, because cooking bored her. She looks for a green pear and some gummy candies for us, she knows we'll be starting to make demands before long. We leave with our few purchases, and outside there's no longer any doubt, night has fallen. The moment has come, the sudden yet expected absence of natural light, replaced by the streetlamps, making her think inevitably about the end of the trip. Since leaving Queens, she hasn't been back to the States. There's something about this place that has a hold on her, she doesn't really know what. Maybe it's the way she experiences loneliness here. Yes, maybe that's it, a country built of the loneliness of millions where hers would just be one more, free of fuss and garishness. She knows she would find a job within a week, she's sure of it. One of her sisters lived in Miami for a while. Her husband was a radio broadcaster, commentating on car races, the Indy 500, things like that. She must still know people who could help her. She sees herself in a one-room apartment, small, well furnished. But if she doesn't go back, she won't be able to give Olga her gift. Olga is her best friend from work. She bought her a special dye, the color of wine, for her hair. Out of nowhere, she's overcome by the desire to go out dancing with her; when they were single they went to the Mamut Rosa or La Pildora. Even though her friend is twenty-five years older than she is, they understand each other perfectly. Why does she get along so well with older women? She wonders what song they might be rehearsing in the office choir. They're both contraltos. He's a baritone. She, Olga, Olguita, married to a Swiss man, last name Abderhalden, was the one who introduced her to her husband. She'd seen him in the hallways while evading a swarm of brokers that trailed behind her, asking favor upon favor. It only took two years for Gloria to make herself essential to that bureaucratic machinery, all under the job title of Secretary to the Director of Interior Customs, a former Army colonel, strict and unpleasant, a desiccated cactus. At the time, it occurred to her that he even looked like Sandro and smiled to herself when a friend pointed it out. They talked a couple times and one random Tuesday, after lunch, he left a dessert on her desk. Then they started going on dates. They were both from the provinces, the difference was that he'd been raised by a single mother, while she'd grown up surrounded by wizened landowners. Now he dresses even better than she does. He buys his clothes from a pair of Avianca pilots who bring it back from Madrid and sell it under the table at a warehouse in Residencias Tequendama where he goes once a week. Everyone thinks he's charming, still. She would come to know his temper, stubbornness, and bitterness much later. And the girls in the office still smile at him with stars in their eyes, she thinks now as we move away from the supermarket after hours of pleasant drifting, life forces us to choose a destination. We turn the corner toward the hotel, where he awaits. From a distance, we see the glowing Monte Carlo sign crowning the top floor. She's mentally packing her suitcase as we approach, no clue where she's going to put everything she bought. She'll have to wait two long years to debut the bathing suit she bought in a boutique. *Boutique, chiffonier, briqué, papel toilette*, terms that stuck with her from studying with French nuns and that she'll never shake. It's a peach-colored one-piece. She'll wear it to swim in the pool at the country house they bought with the Hipódromo money that we'll go to every weekend until we tire of the sun, chlorine, ourselves, and each other. For nearly a decade, we'll go up and down mountains, traverse canyons, slip parallel alongside the rapid Sumapaz River, until at last we descend into a dense heat, all in a matter of hours. The architect who designed the house will sell it to us shortly before my sister's birth. There will be five of us. The day he hands over the keys, they'll invite him to lunch at the Pozzetto restaurant, holding hands, nervous and happy, under the table the whole time, the same table where a week later a killer will sit. And where, after polishing off his third screwdriver, he'll start shooting. The papers will say he was a veteran of the Vietnam War and she'll remember Tigre's cousin. And Tigre, but she won't say anything to him. The country house, a kind of chalet in the middle of the tropics, with exterior walls made of stone and wood ceilings, spacious and comfortable more than luxurious and, above all, full of light. He hates the dark. Amid lizards, cicadas, sunburned and peeling shoulders, and cuts of beef that he'll grill poolside, we'll see artillery helicopters in the sky, coming and going from an anti-guerrilla military base on the summit of a nearby mountain. He'll buy a German pellet rifle with the goddess Diana stamped on the barrel and attempt— but fail—to emulate the duck hunts he went on with his uncle and godfather at the lakes on the outskirts of the small provincial city where he was born, hundreds of kilometers from the small provincial city where she grew up. Chimbilás, those little bats, will skim across the treetops at dusk and frighten her, making her think they're trying to build nests in her hair, ensnaring her in the heat. On Saturday nights, after dropping us off at the movie theater in that town of scorching earth, they'll remain silent or fight, more all the time, while waiting for the show to end. My brother and I will emerge anxiously after seeing *Robocop* or *The Lost Boys* and get into the car that'll move through the night in silence toward the country house, between silhouettes of mango, tamarind, and almond trees, convinced that this discreet routine will protect us from the bombs that soon will start exploding in the city. One of them will destroy part of the office where the two of them work, the building housing official branch offices, located in an industrial area, studded with little windows where faces peer out and hands holding the pink pages of customs manifests can be seen. Its labyrinthine and cool corridors will be destroyed by the 135-kilo dynamite car bomb that a narcotrafficker will detonate in the offices of the newspaper located in the next building. The bomb will blow up on a Saturday, and after a weekend spent relaxing in the pool, she'll find a pile of broken glass atop her typewriter on Monday morning. If she'd been there, typing, it would've been encrusted on her face. For a month, she'll have to work amid the rubble and look out the window at the destroyed roof of the newspaper building and the two columns left standing of a gas station that the explosion wiped off the map.

But it's still a while before all of that and right now, in January 1983, there are just the three of us, my mother, my brother, and me, walking with the warm night overhead. She lets me push the stroller the last few yards and we enter the hotel. The concierge greets her with a slight nod and we take the elevator up to the eighteenth floor. The doors open and the choppy sea becomes visible through a picture window at the end of the hall. The blowing wind has become a gale, a piercing whistle filters in somewhere. Our flight is the following afternoon, so we'll have all morning to pack. We arrive at the room and knock on the door. We're tired after the walk, irritable, it won't be long before my brother starts crying, she knows. Nobody answers. The rum-raisin ice cream, he must be in the bathroom. She waits a moment and then knocks harder, using her wedding ring. She should've taken the room key with her. Could he have gone out? She really doubts it. A third knock, this time openhanded, and only a menacing silence in response. Something's wrong. She's suddenly overcome by a feeling of abandonment, of profound loneliness, an empty boat adrift at sea. I ask what's wrong. Instead of answering, we go down to reception. The concierge calls up to the room. Nothing. We go back up with a bellhop, a young man with a conical torso and a tight belt to keep his pants from falling down. She knocks a fourth time, with annoyance and anxiety. It's possible that he's sleeping, that he disconnected the phone. She looks at the bellhop, nods. The small man takes out a master key and opens the door. The lights are off. She hears a kind of groan from somewhere. She steps back, frightened, and the bellhop enters the room. The main light doesn't work, so he turns on the one in the bathroom. A shape beside the bed comes into view. It's not the luggage or the shopping bags. The shape is moving. Now she goes ahead of the bellhop and turns on the lamp on a table by the door. She sees him gagged, bound hand and foot, eyes shining, the dilated pupils of a newly dead animal. She hurries to untie him. Upon removing the gag she recognizes it as one of the pillowcases. She hears how his breath comes in ragged gasps and only then does she notice the total chaos of the room. She hears him utter clipped phrases. Three of them, two men and a woman, they had a pistol, they took the camcorder and all the equipment. Also one of the porcelain pieces imported from Japan that they bought in the World Showcase, a samurai with a devil mask that would never make it to our living room. The other, a geisha dressed in a blue-and-gold kimono, survived the robbery and will spend years in a corner of our California-style house, which is how it was described in the developer's brochure, located in a neighborhood on the west side of the city, neither in the wealthy north nor in the impoverished south, far from any point of reference. On the way to the airport, I'll say at school years later when people ask, and my classmates' faces will remain blank, because they simply can't place me on the map of their prejudices. The Japanese girl, as she'll be known to us behind closed doors, will become a totem for several years thereafter. It'll make them, her in particular, believe that her desire to flee will fade, that the magma will cool, in the end, that it'll never force the two of them to sign, together, a certificate of collective resignation, and that the money won't start to run out. That bets can last forever. Yes, the Japanese girl will make them think, make us think, that we've done it, that we've made it to the other shore, because that's also what it's about, lying.

The bellhop communicates with reception, relays what's happened. The police will arrive soon. He goes and leaves us alone. Our childish tears are joined by his, repeating like a mantra the camcorder, the camcorder, head in hands. She goes to him. Embraces him, dries his tears with her hands, strokes his unshaven cheeks, he's another child and not her husband. She convinces him that they'll buy the same equipment again, early the next morning. They'll do an overdraft, an advance on their credit card. Then she walks slowly toward the curtain, draws it back, and recovers the porcelain geisha. It was saved because the box it's packed in fell behind the curtain when she closed it before they went out on their walk. She sets it on the bed to his surprise and then turns back to the window and stares out with crossed arms. Out in the hallway, they can already hear the static of radios, the footsteps of the police officers coming to take his statement. A few drops of rain smash violently against the glass. It makes her think of something she heard an Argentinian woman say in the elevator: a hurricane is coming. She stands there, watching the palm trees bend in the wind, serpentine in the dense dark. Instead of being moved by his last sobs, she thinks about the inside of that Porsche, what it might've smelled like.

SHE'S NEVER WALKED THROUGH MIDTOWN THAT LATE.
Whenever she's there on her own, she always returns to
Queens before sundown. And with Tigre, everything is a
race. They've barely finished eating and he's already headed
for the subway, determined to ride it back, afraid of violating
some nonexistent curfew. His justification is always the same:
Things are changing fast, I've seen three robberies, one with
a pistol, he repeats, careful not to tarnish his street-fighter
nickname. But with spring, the city summons its faithful,
arms opening little by little, and she, at twenty years, three
months, and seven days old, is there to answer the call no
matter what happens, she thinks, welcoming a warm gust of
wind on her face as they turn north on 34th Street, one of
those currents that slip between buildings like snakes in the
scrubland. She'll repeat that nighttime walk the next weekend. Say no more. She's adopted that saying of her boyfriend's from having heard it so much. She wants to know if
the orchid vendor is always set up on that same corner they

just passed and if there, farther along, where people are waiting in line, the lemon ices are better than the ones at King of Corona. She could even go up to Fifth Avenue, instead of going along Seventh as they are now, and stop by Raúl's pipe shop and say hi. It stays open late on weekends. A boy looks at a discarded shoe, sole up. He moves it with the tip of his toe while his mother resignedly studies one of the shop windows on 35th Street. Where will they all be in one week? She has to come see if they're still there. Walking is everything, the best antidote for the anxiety attacks that sometimes visit her. She likes how her footsteps sound on the sidewalk. She focuses on each one and they echo even louder when she does. Tock-tack-tock-tack-tock-tack-tock-tack-tock-ta. Carlota's voice reaches her from behind.

"I have to stop for a second at the workshop. They left an envelope in the lobby for my mom."

"But don't take too long. I'm so hungry. I don't think I can wait until Queens. You guys?" Tigre asks, turning his head ever so slightly, like a truck driver who has to keep his eyes on the road. Really, it's a signal for them to catch up. Torero and Carlota answer the call. Now all four of them walk together. They realign, the men, the women. A car runs over a plastic bottle and the resulting pop startles Carlota. Someone, a man, pauses and modestly bends down to spit in the gutter. The saliva doesn't detach entirely, some clings to his chin, and he has to wipe it away with the inside of his shirt. He curses in a low voice, thinking that nobody sees him, but she's there, witness to that minor misfortune that might indicate the beginning of his end. There's blood in his saliva.

"I promise, Tigre, I won't be long."

"Uh, yeah. We could get hot dogs at a cart on Forty-second," Torero suggests, making it clear he's starving too.

"No, no. If we're going to eat, I want to sit down for a while. I'm exhausted," Carlota says, waiting for someone to back her up.

In addition to realizing that the lights are especially dazzling, the whistles shriller than ever, and the buildings seem to loom over her because she hasn't eaten anything since the piece of toast that morning, Gloria sees a perfect opportunity to reinforce her alliance with Carlota—in case they need a united front—and simultaneously restore balance with Tigre.

"What about french fries at Caesar's?"

"And beer! Perfect. Good call, Gloria. Why didn't I think of that? That's it. Let's go. Say no more."

Tigre quickens his pace, forestalling any discussion. They fall in line again. Him-her, her-him. They move through the intersections of 36th, 37th, and 38th, the way rivers are crossed according to the flow of their currents, sometimes cautiously, sometimes boldly. Gloria recognizes herself in Carlos Arturo, they both belong to that category of people who only find meaning living in the city, far from valleys and mountains, standing at intersections, waiting to cross streets, fantasizing about what would happen if they stepped out in front of a passing car.

Soon, Times Square will materialize before her eyes, she can feel it in the air, the way you sense the sea even when it's a mile away. The only difference is that it doesn't smell of brine. But of smog, of perfumes from the farthest reaches of the world, and of the occasional stream of urine left by some drunk. By day, walking, she's been struck that the particles vibrate differently near Times Square, as if they'd been run through a giant atomic accelerator. She can't imagine how it might be at night, some Saturday when the air is seventy degrees.

At 39th Street, a man festooned in dead leaves and pieces of indistinguishable materials staggers in front of the couples, forcing them to step aside to avoid him. They regroup like a hunting party and continue on, content in the knowledge that they are together again for a few yards, until without warning Carlota detaches from Gloria's side and half-runs in the direction of a towering building. Gloria takes a step, feeling an impulse to follow her.

"Don't take too long!" Torero reminds his girlfriend, his shout stopping Gloria from looking ridiculous in front of the two men. Instead, she takes the opportunity to look around.

So this is what it's all about: people buying magazines at kiosks, not caring that it's already ten at night, groups of girls laughing and smoking, couples dressed for a night out, hungrily entering local restaurants. Life . . . is it not a mystery, the greatest of all?, the one and only? she thinks, feeling so much after all those songs and all that time in the streets. She doesn't wish she were dead like her father, of that she's certain. A sob rises inside her, surging from her stomach into her chest. She holds it down, clenching her fists so hard her knuckles turn white. Better to see if Carlota has reemerged from 550 Seventh Avenue. She takes a deep breath, opens her hands, relaxes, and the surge of feeling passes. She turns toward the entrance, toward that building constructed in 1925, and is surprised by its majesty, but even more by the thought that she's been inside it, on a top floor, not in the lobby, as her friend is now, explaining something to the concierge. Number twelve to be exact. Where Oscar de la Renta's workshop is located. Carlota had taken her there for a visit. The Duchess of Windsor is in the dressing rooms, Tito told them, self-importantly, walking briskly by, a tape measure slung around his neck. And of course she remembers how he looked that day, walking self-assuredly through that small fortress, his refuge. Carlota didn't hesitate to turn and follow him, hoping to catch a glimpse of the duchess. Nobody in the workshop was bothered by having Josefina's daughter flitting about.

Sometimes her mother called and asked her for favors, can you take a package this afternoon to such-and-such address, all the messengers are busy and it's very urgent? Carlota never complained. She liked doing those favors, typically the packages were for rich people, living in buildings on the Upper East Side. At the entrance, when she announced that she was there on behalf of Mr. Oscar de la Renta, they ushered her in without hesitation. She rode up in cedar-paneled elevators, walked down corridors with art deco drop ceilings and, upon receiving her at the door and seeing her lazily fan herself with one hand, some offered her a glass of water, especially the men. It was one of them who'd told her about the club—that club. He said he was a fabrics manufacturer. But the important thing was that Gloria got a chance to roam freely around the workshop. She didn't meet the boss of bosses, once she thought she caught a glimpse of his shadow gliding by. Nevertheless, his presence transmitted a sense of absolute control. It was a brand of oppression she knew all too well. She felt it at home in Bogotá, even when her mother was miles away. It was as if gravity shifted inside her and things felt heavier: the telephones, the cutlery, the chairs, even the blankets gained a few ounces. Even so, Gloria felt good walking among the sewing machines, watching a massive woman cut a piece of cloth with scissors, touching the thimbles, the tailor's chalk. She remembered the full-time seamstress her mother employed back home. She made them pajamas, bedding. The only thing she didn't sew them was underwear. It struck her as a noble occupation, feeling like an adult using that word, after touching a purple thread on a big table and rolling it up into a little ball with her fingers. Josefina should help me get a receptionist job there, she said to herself, after discarding the little ball of thread in a trash can. She knew they were looking. Carlota had been offered the position, but she'd turned it down, didn't want to be under Josefina's gaze all the time, which Gloria understood. But what about her? She would be good at it and you never know, she might even end up becoming the designer's personal secretary. She'd already gotten a taste for the city, honey on her fingertips, and she wanted to stay whatever the cost, she decided there and then, in the workshop.

"See, she didn't take long at all. Here she comes," Torero informed them, proud of his girlfriend and how she kept her word, entirely ignorant of what the next weekend would bring. On Friday, Carlota would start working nights as a waitress at a club on the corner of 59th Street and Fifth Avenue and within a month they would probably stop seeing each other.

It's for upstanding gentlemen was the expression her friend used when she revealed her on-pain-of-death secret. Be very careful not to mention it to anyone. You should apply too. I'll help you. They pay way better than the photo lab, she said. And the truth was that she'd considered it, pacing back and forth in her bedroom, perusing the index of the manual the club had given her friend. Read the part about mingling with the patrons, see if I'm lying, but Carlota didn't even let her look. Impatient, she came over, took the manual out of her hands, found the part she was referencing, and gave it back to her, pointing at one paragraph with her finger. Go ahead, she said aloud. Carlota was one of those people who gave orders without realizing it. "Mingling by any female employee with any patron or guest is not allowed and shall be cause for immediate dismissal. Bunnies may, however, converse briefly with patrons, provided that conversation is limited to a polite exchange of pleasantries and information about the Playboy Club. A Bunny may never, under any circumstance, divulge personal information about herself or other Bunnies such as what they do outside the Club, last names, phones numbers, addresses, etc. Bunnies may: have their pictures taken with patrons, provided there is no physical contact whatsoever; dance with patrons at the feature dance party, provided there is no close physical contact (twist, watusi, boogaloo, etc., are examples of acceptable dances)." Carlota repeated excitedly, twist-watusi-boogaloo, moving her hips. A few pages on, Gloria paused to look at a drawing of a girl in some kind of black bathing suit, shoulders bare, impossible heels and eyelashes, bow tie, bunny tail and ears. She would never be able to serve drinks to strangers dressed like that. More than vulgar, the outfit struck her as stupid and infantile. She imagined her friend in that uniform and stopped short of judging her, knowing that, unlike her brother Raúl, ever modest, even shy, reluctant to engage in any activity outside his tobacconist world, Carlota loved attention. She needed it. It nourished her, and if she didn't get it, she weakened quickly, like those houseplants that need water every day. If they don't get it, by the next day they start drooping. It's true, it only takes a little to revive them, but they're always in danger of wilting. She didn't tell Carlota she could get attention somewhere besides that club, maybe because she didn't really know where either.

From a distance, they watch her say goodbye to the doorman with that singular geometric laugh that beguiles and frightens.

"My mom forgot her check. She's so spacey," Carlota says as soon as she gets back to them, envelope in hand, and glances down. Half a second. She does that whenever she's lying. Gloria knows this. It must be the letter of recommendation required by the club, she thinks when she sees Carlota put the envelope in her purse. She must have asked the fabrics manufacturer to drop it off there.

They start moving again, synchronized, a little more slowly, and it doesn't take them long to clash with the

increasingly frenetic rhythm of the city. Faces upon faces,
bodies upon bodies begin to appear, a dance floor suddenly
flooded by dancers who've been waiting all night for that one
popular song.

Out of the corner of her right eye, some red letters catch
her attention, startling her. TE AMO. Just so, in Spanish.
She reads them again. TE AMO CIGARS. She smiles. She
can't help but take the glowing display as a sign. She goes
slightly up on tiptoes and gives Tigre a quick kiss on the left
cheek. He turns, half closes his eyes and returns the gesture,
touching her right cheek with the back of his hand. Then he
whispers something she doesn't catch. They can't stop for an
actual kiss, because the tide of faces and bodies would push
them off the sidewalk. Besides, she doesn't want to miss anything. She hates missing anything. Every twenty, ten, five
yards, depending on the neighborhood, the city shuffles and
shows her a new card: the colossal nose of a deliveryman riding by on a bicycle, the pointy ears of a firefighter, the incon-
solable eyes of an old woman sobbing in a phone booth. Or
a very peculiar way of smiling, like that of the woman right
there, holding hands with a man, approaching, now passing
by. Three young men shout at one another, causing a hamburger to land on the sidewalk. To avoid it, the couple veers
slightly off their trajectory and in so doing, the man's shoulder brushes Gloria, but it's an innocuous brush, the contact

insufficient to merit an apology. In any case, she hasn't focused on his features because she's fixated on the woman's smile. She's seen her before, somewhere, not long ago. She's sure of it. At the fruit stand in Queens where she buys plums? Waiting for the subway at the Jackson Heights station? She turns back, hoping that the woman might have recognized her too and that their eyes will meet in one of those moments of strange intimacy that the city sometimes offers her. She isn't hoping to talk to her, just to confirm that they know each other from somewhere, maybe see that smile one more time. She finds two backs, of similar sizes, a night-sky-blue suit, a clover-green dress. They're holding hands, so tightly that they form a single extremity, an unbreakable chain. Her unanticipated turn forces Carlota, trailing about ten yards back, to stare at the couple, who now pass her by and hurry to cross the intersection, seeing that the 41st Street stoplight is about to change. That's the last thing she sees, a double flash, in perfect synchrony, before her friend asks her, intrigued, raising her voice above the car horns and voices of the crowd:

"Who are they?"

"I don't know . . . I've seen her before. No idea where . . ." she says a little harshly and turns back around to keep from tripping over the trio of young men who are threatening to move from shouts to fisticuffs, and to ready herself to receive the new stream of faces the city is preparing to send her way, but in so doing she realizes that she just lied to Carlota. She does know. She knows exactly who that woman is and where she saw her. Blood pounds in her head, she almost heaves, and her lungs shrivel like a punctured balloon. The problem isn't the woman or her smile, or even the memory of the German shepherd in the bathtub, she's seized by nausea that she suppresses as best she can. The real problem is that she never saw the face of the woman's companion clearly, just catching a vague impression, half an eyebrow. And if there's one thing she needs right now, it's to know what that man looks like, what's in his eyes, because she's certain that he was the one who took the photographs. She turns again but only manages to glimpse the hem of the woman's dress as she enters a department store. She stops, turns around entirely, allowing Carlota to catch up to her, having decided to ask her point blank what he looked like, knowing how good her friend is with descriptions. But after less than a yard, she changes her mind, remembering Amparo's words: they came for the photographs. She decides to wait to hear it directly from her on Sunday morning, giving up for the second time that day. Besides, asking Carlota would force her to explain herself. And she doesn't want to have to explain any of it with Tigre there.

"We're almost to Caesar's. I'm so hungry."

Carlota, slightly disconcerted at the superfluous information, makes a face and answers indifferently:

"Ah, sure, right, almost."

She's filled with disgust, thinking that her shoulder touched that man, the one from the photograph, and by extension some part of the woman and maybe the bristling back of the dog. A rush of blue, red, green, yellow comes to her rescue, telling her to forget about that because they've arrived at the corner of Seventh Avenue and 42nd Street. The 24-hour bowling alley of Times Square is there to greet them. In a trance, everyone, not just her, they turn left and surrender to the molten lava flowing down to Eighth Avenue, which I would say farewell to almost thirty years later, crossing it on my way to the Holiday Cocktail Lounge, a bar on St. Mark's Place, where, of course, Nikki, the Hungarian, took me. The owner of the establishment was a former soccer player from Ukraine named Stefan Lutak who'd bought the place in 1965. That night, my last in the city, I ordered a drink and sat at a table because all the seats at the bar were taken. I kept ordering drinks and thinking about what awaited me upon my return to Colombia, having left without finishing my degree, until a man and two women invited me to join them. I was sick of talking to myself and it was my last night in the city, so I accepted. They were theater students. A director and two actresses. We talked about the owner of the Holiday; they told me he'd fought in the Battle of Stalingrad (My breath turned to ice . . . We slept in the snow for two weeks . . . We had to eat our horses, he repeated sometimes) and had served drinks to W. H. Auden. The poet lived nearby and always sat at the same corner of the horseshoe-shaped bar that Stefan Lutak only left to be embraced by smiling twentysomething co-eds without bras like the ones I had in front of me now. They asked what I did, where I lived, if I was traveling, and after a few seconds, nothing occurred to me but to tell them, half drunk, scrawny and underslept but without a shadow of a doubt, that I'd come to New York six months ago to find my mother and in the end I'd done just that. It was probably in that moment, at that table, that I started writing all of this that I'm writing now.

Fifteen minutes later—the woman's perfect teeth and the man's half eyebrow under lock and key in the basement of her mind—Gloria and the others are sitting at a table in Caesar's. The establishment feels very different than when she'd visited previously. It's not located in a well-lighted area, single women come in from the neighboring bars, men walk out with arms wrapped around each other, and cars roll slowly by, like carriages carrying monarchs surveying their realms. There are beaches of cigarette butts and broken bottles. Sirens ululate sinisterly. At this time of night, it seems like the restaurant transforms into an encampment where noisy groups of men plot their conquest of the night or where old men prowl around on the hunt for some lost bird. She doesn't see the typical families with three or four kids, or the old women talking to themselves with a milkshake and a Bible. Nobody pays any attention to them when they pick out a table, just another four-top of Spanish-speakers.

Tigre is the only one who remains faithful to the idea of french fries. He attacks a crispy double order. The rest of them ordered plain burgers. There are four glasses of beer on the table. Not having to face them while taking big, sauce-dripping bites, he monopolizes the conversation, weaving together a web of phrases that to her ears are just another attempt to make clear that she didn't see what she saw. That her eyes deceived her, projecting a wish onto him and nothing more.

"Clearly, yes, he's the King, that's not up for debate. I would be a massive pendejo to think otherwise, but the issue, at least for me, is that the musicians lacked *verraquera*. In parts, I mean. Not all the time."

"*Verraquera?*" Torero asks, disconcerted, looking up from the burger that he's almost finished, while Carlota and Gloria have only taken a couple bites from theirs. Torero, the only non-Colombian of the group, sometimes struggles to follow certain conversations with terms like *amañarse* or *gallinacear* scattered throughout.

"Yes, *verraquera*. Brio. Desire. Muscle." When Tigre gets excited he has the tendency to fire off gusts of terms he considers synonyms. "Or rather, to put it in a way you'll understand: sometimes the orchestra lacked balls. Sometimes."

"So crude, Tigre," Carlota complains.

"Umm, I don't know, maybe," Torero concedes, and wipes the corners of his mouth with a napkin. He crumples it up and leaves it on top of the two he already used.

"I don't know what you're talking about. I enjoyed all of it, it sounded smooth from start to finish," Carlota says.

"Man, of course, it was great, but what I'm trying to say is that there were times when Sandro was way up here and the orchestra was left behind, deflated. And then the feeling ebbed a little."

"What? Are you crazy?" Carlota says, offended.

"Regardless, the concert was amazing," Torero says.

"I saw you up front, move for move." Carlota shakes her shoulders as she says it and everybody laughs, except Tigre.

"The crowd pulled me up there. And yes, I stayed up front, don't be jealous, I'm not made of wood. The lyrics are pure poetry, but my point stands, the orchestra was lacking, it fell short," Tigre says, defending himself.

"And since when are you a music critic?" Gloria says, and as she finishes the sentence she knows it sounded too aggressive. A silence falls and, to dissolve it before it fossilizes, she quickly adds: "It could've been the sound system or something."

"Yeah, that's true," Torero says, polishing off his burger, crumpling up another napkin, and drinking down the last of his beer.

Tigre is far from letting Gloria's affront slide.

"What the hell is your deal? Quiet the whole time and now you come at me with that?"

"I was just saying it was possible, sorry, I guess."

"Right. Sure," Tigre says, eating a fry and purposefully chewing with his mouth open.

"Another beer?" Torero asks.

"Obviously," Tigre responds, looking him in the eyes, challenging him to get drunk.

"Me too," Gloria slips in, thinking that sharing a second glass will help soothe Tigre. Was it not a night for love? Isn't that what Sandro proclaimed from the stage? TE AMO . . . CIGARS. She should slow down, the first beer was already going to her head.

"I'm good," Carlota says, leaving her hamburger half-finished on her plate.

They order more beers from a skinny and ferocious waitress, a mantis. Dressed in a dirty apron, split ends escaping the hairnet she's forced to wear. Five minutes later, she returns and brusquely sets the glasses of beer on the table. She leaves without a word.

"And what's her deal?" Carlota says, widening her eyes.

"Poor thing, look at this place, it's packed and there are only two waitresses," Torero says and raises his glass to make a toast.

"Well, she should treat people better or there will only be one."

"Salud, my friends. To a great show," Torero says, trying to leave the subject of the orchestra behind.

"Salud!" Tigre responds, dropping a fry he'd just picked up and raising his glass.

"Salud," Carlota says indifferently and feeling betrayed that nobody backed her up in her complaint about the waitress.

"Salud," Gloria concludes.

She's the last to toast, but she clinks glasses first with Tigre and then with the others. Even though she feels a little tipsy, she takes a long drink. Her boyfriend watches her, pleased. They've had drinks together a couple times and she handles alcohol well. That's important to him. It's time for everything to get back to normal. And if she has to tell him that yes, that she invented the thing about him crying so he'll relax, so be it. Who cares. The second beer takes quick effect and she moves from merely talking to dominating the conversation.

"Did you see those theaters? We should come back one of these nights, right? The posters for the movies looked interesting. Apparently they show a lot of films from Europe."

"Okay, okay, some of those films are not for everybody," Tigre says, with no intention of conceding so quickly.

"How do you mean?" Carlota asks.

"Just that, well, let's just say that they are special films."

"With a lot of scenes in bed. Or so I've heard," Torero explains, holding up his hands to clarify that it was third-party information.

"Is that so?" Gloria says, blushing slightly at her own suggestion.

"We could still go," Carlota adds, and smiles as one by one they look at her. She's the leader of a band of thieves proposing they rob a drugstore.

"Yeah, sure. I don't think they're *that* kind of film anyway," Gloria says, exchanging glances with her friend to seal the deal.

"*That* kind?" Tigre mocks her. He sees an opening to get revenge for her humiliating music-critic comment, and he takes it without hesitation.

Gloria snaps right back to avoid looking like a prude:

"I mean, pornographic, in case that wasn't clear," she says, raising her voice to prove to her boyfriend that she's not afraid of the word, not even a little, and upon completing the phrase, the woman in the bathtub comes to mind, a bird circling in a clear blue sky, but she shoos it away with a wave, brave thanks to the alcohol. Someone, a woman, turns to look from an adjacent table.

"How would you know, anyway?" her boyfriend levels at her, and now she's the one left surprised by the aggression. NO TE AMO . . . CIGARS.

"And you do? Someone might think you really know these streets . . ." Gloria says, seriously considering adding information regarding a secret only the two of them know. Tigre immediately understands what she's driving at. It's dangerous terrain and he has no way to defend himself. He has to swallow his anger.

"These fries are delicious. You're not going to finish them?" Tigre asks Carlota.

Changing the subject without disguising it is the only way out.

"No, go ahead." She pushes the plate toward him.

Gloria senses that her friend is going on a diet for her new job. Just then, a pair of policemen enter the restaurant and remove a drunk from the back. They're surprised when he doesn't resist, happy to be carried. Along the way, he tries to kiss one of them. The officer grabs him more forcefully by the arm and twists him completely around, slamming his nightstick into his clavicle. The drunk shrieks in pain.

"We should go back to Queens, it's really late already," Carlota says.

"How about we go to my house and keep drinking. I have a bottle of rum and my uncle and aunt are gone, they went to Newark for the weekend. We could listen to more Sandro."

"Yes, let's go! I want to hear 'Rosa, Rosa' again," Carlota says.

Tigre's eyes light up at the mention of the song that concluded the concert. Gloria wonders if maybe he knows a woman named Rosa and that's why he denied his tears, but then he acts openly affectionate toward her, finishing off his second beer and imitating the song's cadence:

"Gloria, Gloria . . ."

So that's love, an endless game that consists of knowing how to keep your balance to avoid falling into the abyss. She still doesn't know if she likes it; it seems exhausting to stay on top of it all the time. She promises herself that she'll revisit the question later. For now, she tests Tigre—she can change the subject whenever she wants, too. She looks at Torero:

"What would you ask your parents if you could?"

"Here we go with that again . . ." Tigre says under his breath. The hazardous crack that opened a few minutes before prevents him from harpooning her with a more pointed comment.

Torero, an orphan who lost both his mother and father,

raises his eyebrows and leans his elbows on the table, preparing to answer.

"In Spanish?"

"What?" Tigre says without any french fries left to accompany his questions.

"My parents spoke Italian and Spanish."

"Really?" Gloria lunges forward and, a second before she lands on the table, Tigre moves his beer so she won't knock it over, even though there's little danger of that. He can't corner her with words, but he can try to make her look ridiculous.

"They were born in a little town in the south. Furore."

"So you speak Italian?"

"Yes, well, a little. Enough."

Tigre shows interest, not to continue Gloria's game of what would you ask the dead, but because it occurs to him that they could join forces and lead tours in Spanish and Italian. Torero is well-spoken and Tigre has seen the way women look at him. And best of all, he was already complaining about his job at the moving company. He would have to convince his cousin Carlos Arturo. He'd previously suggested that they specialize in excursions just for women. His cousin didn't really consider it. There's a business there, Tigre insists to himself. New York is filling up with women who travel or do things on their own. Or with friends, without men in any case.

"Say something in Italian," Gloria says.

Torero gets nervous and looks to his beer for help, but there's nothing there, just a little foam left in the bottom of the glass.

"Yeah, something. What about that line you fed me recently?" Carlota says.

"Which one?"

"Oh, you forgot already, too bad. When you caught me looking at myself in the mirror at the store. I asked you how I looked in the red dress I was trying on."

"Ah, right. Yes, that line." Torero nods, and you can see in his face how much he'd liked Carlota in that dress. He pauses, takes a little breath. Everyone waits. Putting a hand to his chest, he says ceremonially:

"*Qui è dove le parole muoiono.*"

"And what does that mean?" Tigre asks ahead of Gloria.

"Something like 'This is where words die.' It's from a poem my father liked to recite."

"Bahhhh," Tigre says, and then let's out a laugh so loud that this time it's not the woman but the man accompanying her who turns around. Carlota hates him immediately and Gloria . . . Gloria pales. She trembles, her forehead blooms in little beads of sweat. Tigre notices. He's good at detecting swings in her mood and tries to help when he thinks they're justified or worth paying attention to: "Are you okay? Do you need water? We can go if you want," he says with genuine concern.

"Yeah, yeah . . . I'm okay, it's nothing. I'm going to the bathroom. Get the check," she says, and stands up.

"You sure?" Tigre asks, looking up at her.

"Yes, it's been a really long day, that's all. Probably the beer . . . Getting some air will be good for me. But first I'm going to the bathroom.

She moves slowly between the tables, descends to the lake where death resides, and finds herself leaning against a wall, near the back door. A cook watches her, intrigued. That phrase . . . Could her father be trying to speak to her through Sandro? Or Torero's father?

There's a third hypothesis about her father's murder. She heard it only once, from her aunt, nobody else. Apparently her father might have belonged to the Suicide Club of Armenia, a group of young men from wealthy families. To join, you had to receive approval from the founders and sign an oath. The members gathered once a month to drink and listen to tangos in bars in the red zone of Armenia. In the middle of drinking, they would all write their names down on slips of paper and put them in a cloth sack. In the morning, before going home, the president stuck his hand into the bag and pulled out a name. The chosen man promised to commit suicide. If he failed to keep his word, he ran the risk that somebody from the group would kill him. That was the deal. In the diary that her father left behind, there are various notes about suicide, it wouldn't be surprising if he'd belonged to that club. Maybe he changed his mind at the last second and the Panamanian who shot him, also a member of the club, carried out the sentence, and that was actually the reason she'd lost him when she was barely three years old. On this, she and I agree: her father was the first man to let her down, because letting himself get killed felt like the worst of betrayals.

She takes a couple deep breaths and the cook is about to come over to her, but she collects herself just in time and straightens the scarf she'd wrapped around her neck when they started down 42nd Street. She travels the path back to life and soon is with the others again, en route to the Eighth Avenue subway station. She could never take the subway at that hour by herself and that feels unfair to her.

They continue on their way and she can't stop looking at the multicolored posters for movie theaters the magazines of the day promote like this: "Bryant: large and old theater that used to show softcore movies and now offers hardcore action of acceptable quality at reduced prices. Tickets, $1.95. Love: usually offers new releases or reruns of recent films of varying quality. Clean and comfortable. Now offering live sex shows between screenings. Tickets, $5." Nobody says anything. Even though they're a little tired, nobody dares question the decision to go listen to more Sandro at Torero's house. As they approach Port Authority, Gloria notices that the faces

of the men and women get fiercer, the dresses more extrava-
gant and shorter, the makeup heavier. Across the street, they
see buildings with broken windows and a huge sign: Termi-
nal Bar. At that time of night, the subway is an open trap,
but there are four of them, as young as they'll ever be. They
board the subway car, Queens awaits. Gloria sits down, shuts
her eyes, and is plunged into a damp and heavy blackness.
She's entered a cave. At a certain point, probably while crossing under the river, a deafening buzz floods her ears. Not the
same one as always, it's different, though there's something
familiar about it. She hasn't heard it yet, but she will, years
later, with a third man. In 2005, in the States again, and there
will be nothing I can do to stop it, nothing but accompany her
when the noise ceases.

ON THE WAY TO THE PORT, THE BREEZE COMING DOWN
from the craggy mountains sweeps clean the corridors of
her mind, releases the knots in her neck. They'd reached the
lakes after three hours on the Indian Centennial Chief. Not
one stop, not one complaint. When they left the apartment,
it was still night, just a café con leche and an oatmeal cookie
in her belly, and on the highway connecting New Jersey to
Virginia, daybreak was a while in coming. She almost always
gets tense at first, the exhaust rumbling under her feet, afraid
of falling into the orphanhood that an accident would eventu-
ate, deformed tin, shreds of skin, but it doesn't take her long
to surrender to the pleasure of that pastless world the lines of
the highway offer. On their last trip to Buffalo, she learned
to identify the moment when she could take her hands off
his stomach and put them down at her sides for a couple seconds, next to her legs, feeling the wind between her fingers,
between embarrassed and euphoric. Old jeans and a lined
military jacket is what Gloria wears whenever they go out

on the motorcycle. She thanks him (thank you, thank you, she frequently whispers inside the helmet) for having shown her a form of freedom that'd never crossed her mind to get to know, like something from a television commercial, but not for that reason any less definitive. A true miracle visited on her at almost sixty, three children and a divorce signed and notarized just months before.

At dock number five, in front of the ferry on which they'll cross the largest of the area's lakes, she identifies their tour companions: an Asian couple about their age with opposite styles; three girls in short shorts whom one of the boat drivers with a weather-beaten face remains magnetized to; and a large, loud gringo family that Gloria promises to be tolerant toward. They wait for a few minutes, doing nothing, watching the water be water, the clouds be clouds, the rocks be rocks, until their guide appears. He apologizes for being late, a fight, a minor accident on another dock, nothing serious, he says, raising a fist in the air. She detects a Puerto Rican accent, slightly sorrowful, but Puerto Rican nonetheless. She congratulates herself, she's good at that, like how some people can predict storms just by smelling the air, and then she repeats to herself the conclusion she came to a while back: she likes Puerto Ricans better than Dominicans. Really, the problem is the Dominican women. She dealt with them at Noon & Midnight when she was still a saleswoman. It was the only job she found after giving up living in that twenty-room mansion with an indoor pool in the middle of the New Jersey forest, raising the children of a wealthy Jewish family. Of course she missed the trips to the synagogue, where, to the eternal rage of Mrs. Eva, she was often mistaken for a member of the family. Her mystery, her solemnity. And also on nights when they threw parties and men with impossible bags under their eyes arrived accompanied by elderly, bejeweled women. To avoid being left behind, she put on the diamond ring she was given the day she got married and in that way directed the deployment of tray-carrying waitresses while the owners of the house got drunk. She even missed Jewish Easter, Passover, and the fasting. She was the only one who didn't have to do it. One time she caught Mrs. Eva choking down a turkey sandwich in the garage, hiding behind one of the BMWs, and she had to keep from laughing. But she didn't miss the stone fireplace with the eight-armed candelabra and the voice she sometimes heard issuing from it, a voice in Spanish that for multiple nights had her thinking she'd lost her mind. That was the reason she quit, that and because of the black claw that one of the children, the youngest, asked her to use to scratch his back before he went to sleep. He kept it under the rug beside his bed, and the disgust almost killed her just imagining that stiff and bony thing. No, she didn't miss any of that at all. Nor did she miss the

Dominican women who came next. They always left clothes strewn across the dressing room floor at Noon & Midnight, as if they were in their own bathroom, and nothing made her more furious than having to pick up after them and rehang everything. Either way, she preferred the glowing ember of a bad mood, smoldering until evening, to feeling humiliated and then sad and later lost, like a wounded deer left by the herd to fend for itself. That feeling of abandonment, of profound loneliness, an empty boat adrift, that she'd once felt. He saved her from that with his highway miles, patient hands, and the tickle of his mustache. She'd never felt a kiss like that before, that happy brush of blond bristles against her face. That mustache, his, Mario's, seemed to be pulled taut by two invisible strings every time he laughed and, for some reason, that flooded her with an overwhelming sense of well-being comparable only to sleeping in a bed with freshly laundered sheets.

Frankie, that was the Puerto Rican guide's name, proceeds to inform them when they'll be served lunch and then asks if anyone has any food allergies.

"I can't eat shellfish," she says, shyly, not because of her English, which improved a lot after she was promoted to secretary to the owner of Noon & Midnight, a lingerie shop with twenty locations in New York and New Jersey, but because she knows that people love seafood. Especially if they don't have to pay for it or if it's part of some kind of deal. As it happens, Mario loves it.

"Name?"

"Gloria."

"Gloria. No shellfish," Frankie writes down in a spiral-bound notebook. "Okay, good. Anybody else?"

"I'm a vegetarian. My name is Nancy," one of the three girls says.

"Nancy, vegetarian. Okay. Okay. Got it."

"What's that?" one of the five kids, all boys, that make up the gringo family, asks his mother.

The woman bends down and whispers in his ear as if they were at mass and she were afraid of interrupting the sermon of a vengeful priest. The boy listens to the explanation and then looks at her gravely. Why are you lying, Mom? he seems to be saying with his sparkling blue eyes.

She takes a violet pill from her purse for the seasickness and swallows it before Frankie offers her a hand to help her walk across the narrow hanging bridge and step onto the deck. He offers his hand to Mario too, but he, offended, turns it down and then almost falls in the water. The kids laugh at him, first the eldest and then the rest, one by one, dominos falling, except for the youngest. He just watches silently, punishes and absolves. Aboard the ferry, Gloria discovers a dozen more people who'd been picked up at another dock.

They took the best spots, she says to herself, disappointed. She'd hoped to spend the whole tour alone with Mario, to talk about what they had to talk about, but instead they end up sitting at a table with the Asian couple, near the motor. And then, if that wasn't enough, pretty soon the woman tries to start a conversation. In Spanish. She notices an intermittent, silent Mario beside her. Not hearing him comment on the other passengers is strange, as strange as standing on the bank of a frozen river. It's probably the hunger.

"We're Korean. What about you two? We lived in a little town in Mexico for a long time. My husband was recently transferred to Charleston. We're on vacation."

She translates Mario's sigh: we've got a blabbermouth on our hands. The husband, who has close-cropped hair and is wearing a pair of sunglasses that take up half his face, doesn't say a word, just nods. Gloria knows that the woman expects the same information in return, where they're from, what they do, but instead of encouraging her to extend the conversation with a smile, to get lost down roads there's no coming back from and to have to find an exit herself, she just pretends to listen to her, pretends to pay attention when she's actually thinking about the black dog they saw on the highway. They were entering a town and had to slow down. The animal came out of nowhere and she thought that it would bark at them, that it would snap at them from a few yards away, but what frightened her, what really terrified her, was its pink tongue, a streamer protruding from its mouth. She jerked so hard when she saw the dog, Mario almost lost control. After the slight swerve and that fright, she barely moved a muscle on the Indian for the rest of the ride, which explained the knots in her neck, the stiffness in her legs, the shadowy recesses in the corridors of her mind. She thinks about the exercises recommended for long plane rides and starts rotating her ankles in careful circles. That's what she's doing when—after going on forever about her family in Korea, or that's what she thinks—the woman fires off a point-blank question. Her tone is clearly asking for an answer now.

"How long have you two been together? It'll be our thirtieth anniversary next month. We don't know where we're going to celebrate yet."

What to do with this fount of irrelevant information? Mario crosses his legs brusquely. That's what he does when he feels uncomfortable. Or rests his elbows on his knees. Or adjusts his back. Pronounced movements that might even come off as intimidating, as if he were preparing for a fight. The man, the Korean, notes Mario's reaction and says something to his wife in their language. The woman shrugs, she's only interested in the answer, though she already knows it after glancing at Gloria's hand and not finding a wedding band. Gloria doesn't really know what to tell her, she's the first person to ask that question in those terms. Even though a good amount of time has passed since she moved into Mario's apartment, only once has the word *marriage* come up, all those unsettling vowels that she'd already been through, stones crashing into each other in the throat. He was the one who brought it up a few months ago, giving it a powerful shake, before they left for work, Gloria at the main office of the lingerie chain in Paterson, and Mario at the car dealership he owns in Weehawken. They were eating breakfast. Eggs and arepa. If you want, let's talk in July, after my daughter comes to visit, she answered. Mario had been living in the States since the eighties and was a citizen, even though he'd forgotten a long time ago what the name of George Washington's horse had been or how many stars were on the flag. The issue with Gloria's visa, which was about to expire, would've been resolved within an hour at any New Jersey court, and she would be free from the tachycardia that seized her every time she saw a police officer approach along Bergenline, especially after what happened to the Twin Towers. It was an irrefusable offer from Mario's point of view, residence papers as the ultimate and purest act of love. Girl, you let the moment pass you by, an acquaintance told her, but it wasn't something that could be decided with a half-eaten arepa in hand, and Mario always needed to resolve everything right away. His impatience made her impatient. That morning, he reacted by stiffening his back, rolling his shoulders, and stretching his neck. After holding that position, looking at her for five long seconds, he went back to his scrambled eggs, and the news about Colombia on the radio that, especially on that morning in 2005, left both of them feeling like their mouths were full of crushed glass. July came and went without further discussion. Nothing in August, nothing in September, nor the months that followed either. Gloria considered dusting off the topic on their trip to the lakes, traveling always helped her take a serene look at things, but the Korean got there first, and now it strikes her as ridiculous to say that they're . . . dating? But before she can stammer anything, Frankie appears on the deck with a red megaphone in hand. Attention all passengers, these are the onboard safety rules, which right away he proceeds to explain. He's so thorough that the subject of their marital status vanishes completely and then comes the deafening noise of the motor, the beauty of the little islands in the lake where swans float and the music of REO Speedwagon on the boat, things that make sustaining any kind of conversation difficult.

A quarter of an hour passes amid sidelong glances and bland smiles until the food arrives—plates to share, fish, baked potatoes, salad, and, of course, shellfish—and the men dig right in. They take almost everything. Mario realizes it a little late and with a modicum of guilt passes her an extra piece of fish and one small potato. The Korean man doesn't even look at his wife. The woman spins her plate and lifts her fork to her mouth once or twice disinterestedly. Gloria doesn't eat much either, the pointed question killed her appetite, and she's also worried that the Mareol isn't working. If that's the case, she'll have to make an emergency trip to the bathroom, and feeling sick at the start of the ferry ride is not an option. Frankie brings their drinks himself, Coca-Cola for the women and beer for the men. The Korean man silently raises his glass and everyone returns the gesture. In the opposite corner of the boat, the boy who doesn't believe it possible to live off fruits and vegetables alone is fighting with his older brother. Their grunts attract her attention, that of the Korean woman too. The brothers are like two animals that have been locked up for a long time in a damp and lightless room. At a certain point, without meaning to, the boy knocks over his father's drink and the man, reflexively and without a thought, slaps him so hard he almost hits the floor. Gloria exchanges glances with the Korean woman and, confused and nervous, they both turn back to their plates. Gloria chews a bite of baked potato slowly but can't contain the impulse to glance up searchingly for the boy. Tears run down his face, leaving two gleaming streaks. He must be about eight. He doesn't make a sound, not even a little sob, and instead of taking refuge in his mother—how many times has she betrayed him—he turns his back on everyone and stares out at the lake. He wants to empty it with his eyes. Mario touches her softly and Gloria turns, the Korean man is raising his glass again and he'll do so once more a few minutes later, half drunk, thickening the atmosphere. With lunch finished, they leave the Korean couple to their own devices and head up to the second level, standing there for a while looking out at the dozens of little rocky islands all around them, breadcrumbs scattered across a green-blue tablecloth.

At the halfway point of the tour, they stop at a large island, the heart of the lake. Frankie suggests they all hike up to a lookout to watch the sun set.

"In a half hour, we'll be back at this same spot," he says with a tour-guide smile that vanishes from his face as soon as he exits the frame.

The group, unbearably compact, begins to climb a stone stairway to the lookout. The two of them hang back on purpose. Gloria is incapable of facing more questions. After five minutes of ascending, she pauses to catch her breath and, at a distance, sees Frankie and the vegetarian sitting on a bench, behind a tree spangled with yellow flowers. From one moment to the next, Frankie puts a hand on the back of the girl's neck with studied roughness and gives her a long kiss. She receives it with slack arms, easy, outside herself. Something trembles inside Gloria, like the flare of an oil platform, tongues of flame in the middle of the sea. Tigre, phantasmal Tigre, had also been a tour guide and had also kissed her like that a few hours after their trip to Niagara Falls. It's okay, Mom . . . I whisper to soothe her anxiety and, little by little, it works.

She starts up again, a little more slowly, and already at the lookout, she's greeted by the deafening mating song of the cicadas. Her breathing eases, her eyes water from the breeze, but the water glowing under the sun has a narcotizing effect. As the temperature starts to drop, Mario finally embraces her. The moment only lasts a couple minutes. Then a family appears beside them and a man with gelatinous jowls soon distracts her. There's no Tigre anymore. Faces, those puzzles sometimes of too many or too few pieces, have always obsessed her. It probably all started when she was a girl, when she took great pains to retain the image of her father's face in his coffin, to preserve it after he died. She remembers it perfectly and could draw it if she knew how to draw. One by one she opens the rooms of her memory palace, immaculate, organized with monastic care, and is pleased to find the jowly man's face. And yet she's disconcerted by the fact that he's hand-in-hand with a woman and holding a baby in his other arm.

She has a phrase for what happened with that man: intimate moments with strangers. They circle her incessantly.

On the one hand, strangers lower their defenses and open up to her and there's nothing she can do about it; on the other hand, she often finds herself in situations others might avoid. Not Gloria. Obviously, selling lingerie at Noon & Midnight had presented such encounters with uncommon frequency. By far one of the most intense had involved that man, now chewing on a straw, with his family, staring out at the undulating lake and the boats skimming across it.

The majority of Noon & Midnight's customers were Latinas who came almost exclusively from the same five blocks in New Jersey, men were infrequent and gringos even more so. Bald and with the alert eyes of a hunter, he came in through the door and, without looking at the merchandise, came over to her at the register and announced, "Hello. I'm leaving on a trip tomorrow with my husband and I want to look pretty. It's our honeymoon. I need a new babydoll." She'd just opened the store five minutes before. Maybe the man had been waiting in a café across the street. Gloria hesitated nervously for a second. He's a client, right? And he deserves to be taken care of, she said to herself. And she did: she walked him through the store, which nobody visited at that time of the morning, showed him a few options, evaluating his physique, and led him to the dressing rooms. She remembers in detail the image of the man in the mirror, skinny legs, narrow hips, their shared reflex, two people who've never seen each other before, one half-naked, asking hopeful questions: Does the low-cut red one fit better? He really likes red. Or the black lace one? And what about the pearl white with ribbons? He needed her help, he required it to be happy, so she thought about it for a minute and then, with the honesty of a coffin, said: The black one. Yes, definitely the black one. And to soften her statement, she said a line she'd initially borrowed and later made her own: Say no more. She convinced him. In addition to the babydoll, the man got two pairs of fishnet stockings and one of the most expensive pajama sets. Despite the entirely unanticipated nature of the interaction, Gloria was proud of the sale. A few weeks later, the man came back to the store and gave her a box of almonds with a bow on it as a thank-you gift. We had a great time, we ate everything, we did everything, he told her complicitly, treating her like an older sister, like a lifetime confidante, certain they would never see each other again. And now there he was, four yards away, watching the sun sink into the water with embittered eyes, dried plums, in the company of his wife and baby. An asteroid shoots full-speed across her mind, approaches, and threatens to destroy Planet Gloria: and what if Mario is just that, an intimate moment with a stranger? Slightly prolonged, far more prolonged, but what if that's all it is? Mario detaches from her side and the sudden absence of his warmth lets her know that it's time to climb down from the lookout.

The ferry's foghorn announcing their return to the dock wakes her up. Five minutes, half an hour, she can't calculate how long she's been asleep. As she opens her eyes, Mario hurriedly puts away his cell phone and hands her a bottle of water. From the concession stand, he explains without her having asked. There were a couple vans. Oh, that's nice, is all Gloria can say with her dry throat. She drinks the water in big gulps until a stream spills down her neck, cooling it, she cleans herself off with a napkin, and only then does she look around. Sometimes it takes her a while to come back into herself after a nap, lingering for a few seconds in that limbo where everything is violent or sad. The big family of gringos is nowhere to be seen. Could they have stayed on the island? She imagines them hunting and fishing, cooking over an open fire, and weeks later, the parents dead at the hands of their children, under the command of that boy with rage in his eyes. What a horrible scene; she decides to look for the Koreans as if they were her friends, as if she missed them. They're standing at the back of the boat, waiting to get off. Great, but I hope they aren't going to the cave too, she pleads silently.

Back on land, in a matter of minutes, they grab their helmets from the cubbies and get on the Indian. Before pulling out, Mario goes over the map a couple times and concludes that they are about twenty miles from the hotel. They reserved a cabin in a place that advertised itself as "the ultimate experience of an authentic Amish town." They chose it solely because if its proximity to Luray Caverns and their plan is to go early in the morning. Night falls slowly and on the highway, among semis and buses traveling coast to coast, she imagines a hot shower and high-quality towels. Thin towels make her think of an expression that sometimes came out of her dead-and-buried mother's mouth when she saw a distant relative fall on hard times: *hard knocks*. *Hard knocks*; a way of naming being virtually penniless, dirt poor, down and out. More and more, the music of past words detaches and comes to her at the most unexpected times. More than anything else, aging is the music of the past coming back from far away, *ladies and gentlemen, the only Latin American who has ever performed on this grand stage, with you*, and the realization of how few times she has left to do certain things. Having a limited number of opportunities to see certain people. Mario, many, all of them if they were just to go to the courthouse and sign the papers. How strange, meeting someone at just the point when life narrows like a funnel and starts sliding toward the end and, a little while later, feeling in the shower as if that person will never not be there. How to suspect, how to think that a fleeting encounter between divorcees in a Chilean bakery on Bergenline would lead to an invitation to the movies in Jersey City. And then a date at a Cuban disco and later a midweek breakfast, two breakfasts, three breakfasts, because they can no longer not see each other. And on like that until she found herself sitting on a reverberating high-cylinder-capacity motorcycle, traveling with him, together, the smell of the countryside blending with the smell of gasoline.

Mario was right, the trip was worth it. From above, the caverns feel enormous and intricate, a beautiful wound that they slowly delve into. They walk attentively and reverentially, as if in the room of a patient who recently received a heart transplant. Or through a cathedral. Yes, that's it, the lights, designed to accentuate or contrast with the rocky formations shaped by millions of years of water trickling down from the surface, make her feel as if she's inside a damp cathedral, a living cathedral. They descend slowly and before long they're alone. She reads the names on the pamphlet that they were given at the booth by the entrance. Despite knowing the language, she struggles to understand the words. Speleothems, stalactites, stalagmites. Mario stops and asks for the paper. With his head tilted to one side, an expression she's come to love and one that comes out even when he signs a check, he studies the pamphlet as they listen to dozens of drops of water falling into distant pools. She shuts her eyes. Time doesn't exist outside of that sound, the age of the earth in a sound. Her entire life in that sound.

Little by little, he points things out to her, look Titania's Veil, there's Pluto's Ghost. The Saracen's Tent is her favorite until they reach the Dream Lake. The depth and the height are difficult to measure, the perspective is distorted, it's like being inside a painting, and she's so moved that she takes hold of Mario's arm to share the feeling. They walk for a while like that, arm-in-arm, through the chiaroscuro. If the warmth of his body and his dry-wood smell lost their novelty some time ago, sometimes she finds it hard to believe that she's living what she's living. An autumnal love. She remembers that a journalist used those truly ridiculous words to describe a fleshy Sandro's latest romance. She saw the note on a Latino TV program. It was accompanied by some scenes from the concert she attended almost forty years ago. In the odontologist's waiting room, she sat there thinking about that mysterious tremor of her youth, that irrecoverable vibration that was perhaps extinguished that same night, after what happened happened. She's never told him that story, the story of Tigre. She's going to now, she's about to, she's ready . . . Mario, you'll never imagine, I never told you that when I was twenty, I went to Madison Square Garden with some friends to see Sandro, we were there, right up front, we could almost touch him, it was incredible, someone even wept with excitement, and afterwards, we walked to Times Square, in those days, it was different, dangerous some people even said, and we ate french fries and drank beer at Caesar's. But that's not the whole story. Later, back in Queens, we went to one of our friend's houses to keep partying, we were so happy, but at the end of that night, early in the morning really, something happened, something that I swear, I swear to you that I . . . She's left with the story stuck in her throat, because Mario urgently needs to get outside to catch his breath. I need to go outside to catch my breath, he says. The cave's ceiling has gotten lower and lower to where it's only about a yard above their heads. Claustrophobia. He used to suffer frequent attacks and that's partly why he started riding a motorcycle, he confessed to her the first time he showed her the Indian, one Sunday, the first of many when he went with her to dismantle the small stand she rented in Braddock Park. Mrs. Eva and her millionaire friends had given her tons of designer clothing that they no longer wore and Gloria had the idea of selling it at a flea market. She became famous among the twenty-something women; she was the woman who sometimes wore a short Chanel jacket or Gucci heels. Or an Oscar de la Renta miniskirt. At the end of the afternoon, Mario would help her put what she hadn't sold into two large suitcases and then take her out to eat. One day, he suggested that they spend their Sundays riding his motorcycle instead of at the flea market and away they went. Are you okay? Yes, yes, it's nothing, but better . . . Mario says and gestures with his hand to wave away the seriousness of the attack. She wants to continue walking. I'm going to keep walking a little longer, she says. They agree to meet outside, in fifteen minutes. Alone, Gloria reviews the pamphlet again and on the third page, she sees something that she immediately wants to check out. She walks through a couple of times, but she's so bad at figuring out where she is, she fails to locate the spot even though she can hear sounds coming from that part of the cave. There's nobody around. A menacing shadow is cast in the distance. Better to go back, maybe I'll convince Mario to come with me. We can't leave without seeing that. We have to see it. The natural light guides her to the exit ahead of when she was supposed to meet him, a rope she slowly climbs into the outside world. Upon emerging, she doesn't find him, but she hears his voice, how strange, he seems to be talking on the phone to someone. She finally locates him, twenty yards farther along, leaning against a wall of stone. He's covering the receiver with his hand; it looks like he doesn't want them to hear him. Gloria moves closer and only then, because of some effect of the acoustics, does his voice reach her clearly. She feels guilty for spying on him, but his words sought her out, not the other way around, the point is that she starts hearing them one by one until, as they begin to arrange themselves into sentences, she can't stop. I already explained it, it's not easy, we've been together a long time. As soon as she's out of the apartment, you'll come from Chile. Be patient, please . . . Her immediate reaction is to turn around and retrace her steps, aghast at the monstrosity. Back in the cave, she plunges into the dense, damp darkness, she's in a subway car, eyes squeezed shut, crossing under the water of a river when she was twenty years old. A deafening buzz fills her ears and then she's overcome by an excruciating and expansive palpitation but remains horrifyingly lucid. If an animal could be aware that its viscera had been ripped out and it'd been hung from a hook, it would feel like this, like how she felt. She pushes farther into the cave, hoping it'll devour her, and, without meaning to, winds up in the place she was trying to find before. In the middle of a gallery, she sees it. She read in the pamphlet that it runs on electricity and produces sound by touching stalactites of different size with a special mechanism. Empty and defeated in that cathedral of stone, with her hands made termites, she moves toward the organ, but before she reaches it, she thinks she hears a sob from behind a huge column. Or is it that she's weeping without realizing it and the echo is sending her spasms back to her? She glances to one side. Someone comes out from behind the column. They recognize each other. The Korean woman wipes her face with the backs of her hands and comes toward her.

"It's over. Thirty years. That's what he said, it's the end . . . The end."

Before she drops to the floor, Gloria steps in and catches her. She doesn't say anything, just holds her, feeling the

Korean's hollow bones press against her own. She focuses for a long time on the other woman's pain to avoid her own, which she knows she'll have to deal with for weeks, until I arrive at the beginning of winter to keep her company and live with her amid snowstorms and trips to the laundromat. A sound startles them and the embrace is broken. Behind them, the organ has begun to play halting notes. She's heard the melody before, it's one of those pieces of classical music that gets played so often it becomes a popular song. They go over and discover that the person playing the organ is the boy. The boy with sparkling eyes, full of rage. Without turning to look at them, he starts the song over but this time glides confidently across the keys, playing as beautifully as he'll ever play. It's the first time in his life that he's gotten the tune right, and the two women are his only witnesses. Gloria doesn't know at what point she grasped the Korean woman's hand. Watching the boy play, she feels that the three of them are a family. A family of strangers that the others, with their cowardice, with their malice, have tried to bury beneath that cathedral of water and stone.

●

TORERO'S APARTMENT ISN'T JUST MUCH BIGGER AND older than Josefina's, it's also full of furnishings inherited from other immigrants, relatives and strangers, except perhaps for the coffee table, which appears to be new. She's in front of it, sitting on the edge of the sofa that her host offered to her with an open hand, barely showing his palm, without a word. She bends down to pick up a button and sets it on the table, beside the Sandro albums. She can't stand seeing things lying on the ground, she always has to pick them up and put them on top of something. Sometimes she struggles when she finds buckles, gloves, batteries in the street. Buttons. To tell the truth, if given a choice, she would've preferred to sit in the armchair next to the radio. Carlota and Torero are in the kitchen. She listens to the couple talking. They're looking for glasses, ice, a bowl for peanuts. Gloria is still hungry. And what about them? Are she and Tigre still a couple? Is she still his girlfriend? When she sees him, she knows she is, but when he's not there, in front of her, she's not so sure anymore. I won't be long, is what he said. Tigre. He was going to get a turntable, to borrow it from a friend who also lives in Queens, not far from there. My aunt and uncle's is broken, Torero remembered half a block from his apartment, and the plan to listen to Sandro was almost canceled. But like so many times before, in a matter of seconds, Tigre came up with a solution. That's his specialty: resolving issues, straightening out situations, covering up problems. They said goodbye to each other with a quick kiss, neither of them wanting to extend it. And if she moves to the armchair? No, that would be an affront. She slides away from the edge of the sofa, leans back, and is surprised to find how comfortable, how welcoming it is. It's the first truly pleasant sensation she's had in hours and she takes a moment to savor it. Thank you, Torero. She feels indebted to him and repays him with her next thought.

I was the only one who arrived on a plane, he'd said, coming up the stairs. His aunt and uncle left Furore for Naples and then Naples for New York and his parents left Furore for Rome and Rome for Montevideo, promising to find each other as soon as possible. The families fell apart in one night, Torero smiled bitterly, keys in hand, with that philosophical vein that he sometimes reveals. His parents lasted decades separated from his aunt and uncle but died when they finally decided to make the jump to Queens. Two heart attacks in less than a month, one after the other, and Torero was left more alone than zero, that's how Gloria imagined him on the landing, before he opened the apartment door, and she felt sad for him. She's come to the conclusion that people don't know how to feel sad, so she helps them. Feeling sadness for others is her specialty, according to Carlota.

Torero was the latest arrival to that place so many others had lived in, because it wasn't just a collection of furniture that'd ended up there, she thought, looking around the living room with one foot on the doormat, as if they'd washed ashore on an island following a shipwreck or a hurricane. And those windows, covered with heavy curtains that the dust had clung to until it turned them a light brown. It was possible that the house's inhabitants feared their souls would escape if they opened one. Which takes her immediately to the wet-bread smell that she perceived as soon as she set her other foot on the doormat. Sometimes someone gives off a similar smell on the subway, almost always an old man who one fine day decided to put on an old jacket that'd been stashed away for years, maybe since the last war. She has also smelled it in waiting rooms, and in corners of stairwells, and emanating from the hairpieces of certain bank tellers with whom she's shared an elevator. Even in some songs. She swears that some songs have that smell, and it's not the hymns the faithful sing in the churches. Without going any further, there are days when Amparo smells like that. The smell, that smell isn't unpleasant, the way an ice cube melting in a dish or a cloud scudding quickly away can't be unpleasant. Just menacing. The smell of no future. And that's the issue: in these moments, Gloria can only think of the future.

From her newly attained comfort, what a delightful sofa, staring fixedly at one corner of the ceiling or at the doorframes, she attempts to trace entire generations of the immigrants who passed through that place prior to Torero's aunt and uncle, and Torero himself. Under the wallpaper, she imagines inscriptions, marks, words in different languages, tongues she'll never recognize. The dark wood floor, varnished innumerable times, more clearly betrays all those past lives. Scratches made from moving a heavy piece of furniture, a board left half broken after the weight of a hammer came down on it, a stain of methylene blue spilled during a fight between siblings or to-the-death enemies. Now that she thinks of it, it looks like a place that the industrial revolution never touched. It could well be lit by candles. By contrast, Josefina's apartment, small and functional, she repeats it constantly, has all possible household appliances, latest model, purchased at the Chevys in Queens. The sum of *modernity*, that word Gloria doesn't entirely understand but has made her own, seeing in the morning, before leaving for Agfa, the blender, the toaster, the coffeemaker, the vacuum cleaner, the television, and the sound system, signs that all is well, that progress is synonymous with consumerism. For Josefina, modernity is also being convinced that the apartment where she lives began and will end with her, as if nobody else had ever inhabited it, as if nobody else ever would. Just the opposite of what's going on in Torero's apartment. Just the opposite of what she feels in her mother's house, that open tomb she hopes never to return to.

Torero materializes in the middle of the room:

"With ice and Coca-Cola? Or just ice?"

He's no longer the boy who approached Carlota one afternoon in the pizzeria. Now, as he moves through the house, he ages in front of her in a minute that contains a year. His uncle and aunt will die, his cousins will marry, and he'll be the one who lives and also dies here. Without Carlota. That's what Gloria thinks; yet she's completely mistaken. After her friend leaves him, she's right about that, Torero will retain his nickname for years, right up until the day he gets shot during a police raid in Montevideo, where he'll have returned to join an underground guerrilla cell.

"Coca-Cola. No lime. Gracias, Torero."

How many people might have said goodbye or passed away in that old apartment? she wonders, watching him pass in front of a washbasin in the most poorly illuminated corner of the living room, apparently unusable, that for some reason had never been removed. It's quite likely that, before having a shower, the inhabitants of that house had no option but to get a cloth wet and wash themselves right there. She imagines them scrubbing their faces and armpits, washing their hands. Hands with traces of foam under a weak stream of water, a piece of porcelain, an almost used-up bar of soap. The memory is ethereal at first and then assumes weight and clarity. Until that moment, she'd believed that the only memory she had of her father was of his burial, when they'd lifted her up over the edge of the coffin, clutching the little purse with a puppy stitched on it that he'd given her a week before he was killed. But no, his silhouette enters their Armenia house at lunchtime. The briefcase and the hat end up on a chair at the end of a long hallway, then she sees him walk toward the main courtyard. The silhouette reddens as soon as it's touched by the midday sun, the same sun she's soaking up on a blanket. He approaches, bends down, and tousles her hair, and then he goes over to the washbasin, beside some pots with flowers the color of blood, the blood soon to spill from him. The foam under the weak stream of water, the piece of white porcelain, the almost used-up bar of blue soap in his hands, the sunlight illuminating them. Her dead father's hands. Something tells her that all of that happened on the exact day that he was shot and that that tousle of her hair was his goodbye. It's not much, but it's enough to step in and impose itself, and when she thinks of him now she doesn't immediately think of a twisted mouth with a piece of cotton protruding from it that the person who prepared the corpse failed to conceal. There's nothing else she would ask him. No need to go to Amparo's on Sunday morning. Her memory has added another layer. She feels the memory settling inside her—calm, like the dust accumulating in Torero's house—so she can share it with me on a winter's night, a few months after she moves out of Mario's apartment, when we're taking blankets out of a washing machine in New Jersey, when she's almost sixty and I'm a little over thirty.

"Raúl asked why you haven't been back to the shop," Carlota says, pulling her abruptly out of that sunny courtyard from her childhood and offering her a glass containing a caramel-colored beverage. Gloria accepts it without entirely returning to that night of the concert, to that spiderweb city. She takes a long sip. Her palate and her tongue shiver, she scrunches her nose, closes her eyes. She forgot that it had rum in it.

"Too strong?" Torero asks from the armchair.

She doesn't know when he appeared in the living room, the way that Korean woman and boy had appeared in a cave when she was riding the subway back to Queens. She was dozing on Tigre's shoulder and opened her eyes at one point, frightened, thinking that some dreams are just things that haven't happened yet, premonitions.

"No, no. It's good, don't worry."

Carlota stands there waiting, one arm across her chest, taking little sips from her glass so that the lime doesn't touch her nose. Her friend likes rum with ice, Coca-Cola, and a slice of lime.

"Raúl . . ."

"Ah, yes, Raúl. I mean, I don't know. Isn't he really busy with the wedding stuff? I'd rather not bother him."

"A little, but my mom and Mary's mom are taking care of the most complicated things."

"Is it going to be in August after all?"

"Yeah, August, toward the end. The boss is going to make the dress for the bride as a gift."

"Oscar de la Renta."

"Yes, they already took her measurements," Carlota says derisively.

Her friend finally indicates that she wants to sit. Instead of coming over to her, as Gloria expected, given the free space on the sofa, Carlota turns slowly around, walks over to the armchair, and sits on Torero's lap, who welcomes her, adjusting himself to better disperse their shared weight. The two of them clink their glasses together and then include her. Gloria takes another sip, more cautious this time, and sets the glass down on the coffee table, thinking that the ice is going to melt and might stain the wood, because she doesn't intend to drink any more. At least not until Tigre gets back.

"He told me that that old man from Sixth Avenue had asked about you."

"Raúl? What old man?"

"Yes, Raúl. Are you really tired or something? You look out of it, in the clouds . . . Sandro still got you down." Carlota laughs at her own comment and then explains to Torero instead of addressing her friend: "He's this very odd old man, always dressed in the tunic and hat of a . . ."

"Viking," Gloria says.

"Well, he always looks like a Roman soldier or something to me."

"Viking. I asked him."

"Homeless?" Torero asks with interest.

"No! He's not homeless." Gloria's back tenses with her response.

"And where did you say he hangs out? On Fifth Avenue?"

"No, on Sixth, Sixth Avenue. Between Fifty-third and Fifty-fourth. Really close to my brother's pipe shop."

"Carlota, when am I going to meet Raúl . . .?" Torero says, suddenly serious.

Carlota has fallen into her own trap by mentioning Raúl, so instead of answering, she leans down and gives him a quick kiss on the mouth. The annoyance that might have remained as such, as annoyance, if she hadn't kissed him to shut him up, spilled over like the foam of a badly poured beer. Torero skillfully lifts her off him. Carlota has to catch her balance to keep from falling with the glass in her hand.

"I'm going to the corner to buy ice, there's none left," he finds himself obliged to explain, even though they know why he's reacted with such anger. For some reason, Carlota doesn't want to introduce him to her family. It's a step she doesn't plan to take. Torero disappears into the darkness of the hallway.

Still standing, Carlota exaggerates her confusion, but soon realizes her stupidity. When she hears the door shut, Gloria asks:

"Do you think he suspects something?"

"About?"

It infuriates Gloria when Carlota treats her like an idiot.

"What else? About that club where you're going to work," she says with a wave of her hand. It came out more forcefully than she intended.

"Oh, no, I don't think so. Nobody knows about the club," Carlota answers, staring at her, including her especially in that nobody.

"Are you going to end it with him?"

"No. Not now. We'll see how things go. And what about you and Tigre? I saw him at the concert."

"You saw him, too? What did you see?"

"Of course, how could I not, he had tears streaming down his face like a little boy. It was impossible to miss."

"That's good. For a minute there I thought I'd lost my mind."

She rests easy, feeling the dead star that she's carried over her heart all night disintegrate.

"Why do you think he was crying?"

"I don't really know," she says, wondering if she should tell Carlota what those tears had made her feel, the possibility of a future together, sensing an unknown Tigre, a better Tigre, in her view.

"You should ask him."

"No. No. I half-mentioned something to him when we were leaving the concert and he got really stormy. And you saw how aggressive he was at Caesar's later on. I think that him making me wait right now, it's part of his revenge. You know how he gets sometimes. That's it, a little boy. A strange little boy."

This would be the perfect moment to tell Carlota what'd happened, to tell her that when it was still cool at night, Gloria went with Tigre to 42nd, the same street the four of them had walked down a little while before. She'd dropped off a pair of shoes to be fixed at a place in Jackson Heights and she wanted to see if they were ready to be picked up. They'd already gotten messed up once. The phone call took less than two minutes. She went into a phone booth, dialed, and asked. Yes, they were ready, they told her. When she hung up, she

turned around and discovered that her boyfriend was nowhere to be seen. The phone booth was right in front of a
small bookstore, Keystone Books. She decided to go in to see
if he was there. She looked for him among the shelves. Nothing. Maybe he went to buy a lottery ticket at the corner store.
He bought one every week. She went back out onto the street,
scanned her surroundings, and found herself focusing on the
place next door. Black Jack Exotic Books. Another bookstore, but the display windows were covered and there were
drawings of women in bikinis. She knew what *exotic* meant
in Times Square. Not caring, she walked decisively through
the door. All the customers and even the clerk turned to look
at her. It was quite likely that a twentysomething woman had
never set foot in there. She found Tigre in the back, flipping
through a magazine. She walked slowly across the entire shop
amid murmurs, and when she had him in front of her, she
told him loudly that she would be waiting for him outside.
That if he didn't come out right now, she would leave. Tigre's
ears reddened. Gloria turned and walked back to the door
even more slowly, knowing how uncomfortable her presence
made all those men. At first, the bookstore hadn't struck her
as particularly scandalous, it was just something that didn't
interest her, like the space race or kimonos, to give two examples, but after what happened in Agfa, everything assumed a
darker valence. The pictures of the woman and the dog could

be there, printed in one of those magazines. Why had he done something like that? Why had he gone in there to look at naked women when he was with her? In the balance of love, she told herself, lying, seeing him cry in public compensated precisely for that.

"Exactly, he was being impossible in the restaurant. He turned into a tiger over something you said!"

Both of them laugh at the easy joke just as Torero comes back in. Alone. Without Tigre. He hears them and thinks that the joke was at his expense. He doesn't greet them and goes right into the kitchen. Carlota knows she has to calm him down or the night will end in a fight.

"My love, are there more limes?"

"No. There was just one in the fridge," he replies curtly.

Carlota turns to look at Gloria, asking for her help.

"Should we put on some music? The radio at least?" Gloria asks.

"Sure," Torero says, less gruff this time. "Go ahead. Turn it on."

Gloria moves as if to get up from the sofa, but Carlota stops her. She's the one who goes over to the radio, turns it on, and searches without hesitating for the right station, the station she wants, the salsa station. A boogaloo was playing. Torero comes out of the kitchen with his glass full of rum and Coca-Cola and Carlota goes to meet him, dancing slowly. For a second, Gloria imagines her doing the same steps at the new club where she's going to work, knowing she would be worshiped. Maybe it's a good job for her friend, maybe it won't be full of those handsy men who sometimes grope them on the subway, maybe the men who went there were upstanding, as she herself said, even though she knows that word is just a shell. Or worse, that she has happen to her what happened to Gloria before she started working at the Agfa labs. She lasted one day as a maid in a hotel in Astoria. So young . . . you don't have a boyfriend?, you don't have anyone?, a man said, approaching her, and those words still crawl up her ankles like cockroaches when she recalls them. Good thing the man was so drunk that a forceful shove was enough for him to fall down on his back in the bathtub and for her to take off running across a room with wicker chairs and many-colored cushions strewn across the floor.

Torero can't resist the dance, and when they meet in the hallway, he puts a hand on her back and then lets it slowly slide down to her waist. He dances a little, feigning anger he no longer feels. The boogaloo continues and he, far more modest than Carlota, at least in front of Gloria, cuts it off discreetly. They separate.

"And what's going on with Tigre? It wasn't supposed to take him long."

"I don't know. It's strange, right? He said it was just down the street and it's been a half hour," Gloria says, sinking into the sofa. The question, and above all her own response, obliges her to take a sip of her abandoned rum. The half-dissolved ice cubes make the alcohol more digestible.

"Where's the bathroom?"

Carlota points to a door in the back. When she stands up, she gets a better look at the Sandro record she likes best of all. She hopes they release one of the concert, her screams among so many others. She shuts the bathroom door and sits on the toilet. She doesn't have to pee; she just wants a little silence. It's a very different space from the rest of the apartment, with that boat-shaped bathtub and wall-to-wall mirror. If she lived in that house, she would spend hours and hours shut in there, but there's something missing, she's not really sure what. That's it, the metal thing that surprised her even more than the automats, the Manhattan restaurants where there are no waiters. People insert a coin and remove a steaming plate from a metal cupboard and that's that. In her apartment, the contraption, which doesn't require the magic of wiring and electricity that Josefina so adores, is beside the toilet, next to the paper. A sanitary napkin dispenser. Sometimes, when she's brushing her teeth at night, she looks at it and it speaks to her of a world that in her mind takes place only in New York.

Outside, she hears broken laughter, the creak of furniture,

a stifled cry. Maybe a vase caught in the nick of time. She doesn't give it much attention and instead removes her shoes. She has this obsession: she can't wear shoes in the bathroom. She leaves them in a corner, stretches her legs, picks up a *Life* from the magazine rack and flips through it disinterestedly. Near the middle, she sees him. His image takes up half a page of the most famous magazine in the world. The gray beard down to his chest, the olive-green tunic, and the red wine cape, bare legs, muscular, some kind of leather satchel, sandals, and a two-yard-long lance. She starts reading the article that accompanies the portrait with the shaky hands of an alcoholic before his first drink of the morning. She can already understand short snippets in English, unlike Tigre, who can't even ask for a discount in stores without her help. The first day she saw him, saw Moondog, that was his name, what a strange name, she didn't have the nerve to ask if he'd been born blind. Now she knows that he wasn't, that when he was sixteen years old, he found a stick of dynamite on the train tracks, started playing with it, and it exploded in his face. He never recovered his eyesight and had to attend various schools for the blind around the country. He learned music theory in Memphis using braille, and in 1943, he took a bus to New York, the Jerusalem of the twentieth century, a city you have to visit at least once in your life, the journalist writes, and Gloria smiles to herself, it's a pilgrimage that's fulfilled the destiny she always longed for. For five dollars a week, he rented a room on 56th Street where he still lives with a sleeping bag, an electric stove, and a portable organ. Four years later, he adopted his name, Moondog, in honor of his childhood pet, a dog that howled at every full moon. For almost a decade, he attended rehearsals of the New York Philharmonic, invited in person by the director, who'd seen him play and sell his poetry on the same corner where Gloria met him. His outfit began to include a helmet with horns to protect his head from the metal signs and streetlights. Besides, he didn't want people to compare him to Jesus Christ or to call him a monk. She stops for a second and thinks about Raúl. He was the one who took the picture on Sixth Avenue in which she appears sitting on a wall in front of a building, beside him. Beside Moondog.

There are no sounds coming from outside. She tenses up, thinks something's happened. Without thinking, she tears out the page, careful not to ruin the portrait, folds it twice, and puts it in the right pocket of her skirt. She leaves the magazine in its place and puts on her shoes.

There's nobody in the living room. Empty glasses on the table, records in their sleeves; beside the radio, the diadem that Carlota had been wearing. The door to the bedroom at the end of the hall is shut. It wasn't before. To keep from having to choose her next step, she despairs, arms outstretched overhead, fingers interlaced. She's afraid of getting a cramp and lowers them quickly. It's almost midnight, the living room clock tells her, and he still hasn't come back. Twice in one day. There's only one explanation for this second absence: an anxiety attack. Who knows what triggered it this time. They're not as bad as the ones his father—a widowed accountant—gets, where, Tigre told her, he could go two or three days without speaking to anyone and only eating plums the entire time. For him, for Tigre, he just gets waylaid by a sense of hopelessness, an unease in his mind, and then he abandons a party without saying goodbye, takes off from a bar without paying the bill, or hangs up the phone midsentence. And to think that, for a moment, it'd occurred to her that today was the day, the night, to have taken him into one of the bedrooms in the back, like Carlota and Torero. But he wouldn't have gone with her to the bedroom, not that night, not yet, because let's imagine, it's all about imagining, that one Christmas, when he was thirteen, Tigre was celebrating with his family and someone, startled by the explosion of a firework, knocked over a gasoline lamp by accident and a burning stream of the liquid splashed across his chest. A doctor friend happened to be on the scene and knew exactly what to do. But he still ended up with a scar that ran diagonally across his chest, from left nipple to navel. A whiplash of fire. There's no other explanation for why he has a shirt on in the pictures where they appear together on a beach near Elizabeth, New Jersey. Tigre is embarrassed by that scar. He's built his whole life on overcoming the furrowed mark and still hasn't been able to.

The comfort of the sofa calls to her, doing what it can to seduce her, but Gloria remembers that there's no future in that apartment and doesn't want to be trapped there. What does she do? She runs.

Less than twenty yards from the entrance to her building, she stops. Her stomach groaned so loudly she thought it was a sound coming from the trash can. It's a complaint about the stretch of days in which she ate poorly, thinking about the concert. John's is open until midnight on Fridays and Saturdays. She has twenty minutes. It's not far, three blocks in the opposite direction, and the worst thing that could happen is that she would run into Tigre sitting in front of a cup of cold coffee. She turns around and starts walking. Not a soul is visible in the streets of Queens. A few windows are illuminated, a wide shadow slides across a bedroom. She hopes she doesn't see a black cat; sometimes she thinks they're about to stand up on two feet and start talking to her. Halfway there, in front of the neighborhood supermarket, a van zooms by at full speed and sends a newspaper flying. She quickens her pace. In the distance, she sees the sign for the pizzeria.

She goes in and sits at the bar under the twinkling lights and the monotone hum of a refrigerator. There's no music playing and for that she's grateful. Enough music for today. The shift worker doesn't recognize her, so she has to order. She does so assuredly, *Cheese, please.* Apart from the man, a blond ravaged by the acne of youth, there's only one other customer. She's sitting at the other corner of the bar, a glass of water in front of her. The pizza arrives, steaming. She sprinkles it with a pinch of oregano. She eats quickly, blowing on each bite with urgency. At times she has to hold her mouth open and half-chew to let the heat escape. When she's almost finished, the other woman gets up from her seat and comes over. She's on the shorter side of average height. She could be Colombian. She sits down beside Gloria without a word. She just stares straight ahead, forearms resting on the bar. The employee tenses up, but Gloria is so tired she only thinks about leaving. She takes her last bite of pizza and leaves the charred crust on the plate. She wipes her face and hands with a napkin and is preparing to pay when the woman glances at her plate and asks in Spanish:

"You're not going to eat the rest?"

She doesn't eat the crust because Carlota told her you weren't supposed to, that's the only reason. Sometimes she abides by silly rules and knows it.

"Umm, no."

"May I?"

She doesn't want to answer but has to.

"Go ahead . . ." She pauses briefly and chooses her words carefully. "If you want, I can buy you a piece. There's still five minutes before they close. It's really good."

The woman bursts out laughing, the violent laughter of someone who has been overcoming pain forever. Then she picks up the crust and starts eating it. The employee spills some of the coffee he's drinking on himself.

"Relax. I have money. I just can't stand when people leave food on their plates. It's just a thing of mine."

Gloria laughs and extends her laugh intentionally, giving herself some time. Best just to confess.

"I have an idiosyncrasy too. I can't pee with my shoes on. I have to take them off whenever I sit on the toilet."

During the mid-eighties, pregnant with my sister, she'll have another obsession. Riddled with a monstrous anxiety, she'll eat little pieces of dried cement whenever she goes to see how the construction of the swimming pool is going at that country house where we'll spend our vacations. She'll stash them in her purse and occasionally stick a hand in and chew them on the sly, as if they were cookie crumbs. And later, when on one Friday she has to go to the emergency room because of a terrible pain in her lower back, on the left side, and they diagnose her with kidney stones, she'll feel guilty but won't be able to tell anybody, not even a stranger in the middle of the night. And even guiltier when for a few months she ends up getting addicted to Demerol, an opioid they'll give her to control the brutal pain that won't let her sleep. One night she'll get out of bed and, under the effects of the drug, look at herself in the mirror. She'll discover an aqueous film on her pupils, a glow of emotion.

"Well, it's not like I go around picking up scraps of food and cleaning plates in restaurants either. But I've seen you before and it didn't embarrass me—or gross me out—to ask. You're always so well put together. Colombian, right?"

"You know me? From where?"

"I work at Agfa. Ecuadorian."

"Really? In what department?"

"In developing."

"Oh, no wonder I don't recognize you, I never go in there."

"I always see you with Amparo. La Capitana, that's what we call her in developing. I'm Lucrecia. Lucre."

"Gloria. Nice to meet you." They shake hands and the employee relaxes a little bit, they're matriarchs of a clan sealing an alliance.

"La Capitana is famous in our department. Clairvoyant. A spiritualist."

"Yeah, that's what she says . . . Honestly, I don't really know." And she remembers that she'll have to call her early in the morning to cancel her appointment. Her father will stay silent.

"Hey, I'm really sorry."

"Sorry?"

"About those photographs . . . you know, Agfa. You hear about everything really quickly at the laboratory, especially about that kind of thing."

Gloria doesn't say anything, feeling sad all of a sudden.

"I worked in shipping for a while, then they transferred me to developing. It happened to me, too. Sheep. With multiple men, in a corral."

"I think I saw them today."

The words come spurting out, like when the water supply is shut off and turned back on after a couple days.

"Who?"

"The woman from one of the pictures. I recognized her from her smile. And the man who took the photo. I'm sure he was the photographer."

"Where?"

"On the sidewalk, in Manhattan, near Forty-second."

"How was he dressed?"

"Blue suit, impossible to forget. She was wearing green."

Lucrecia smiles and shakes her head. She turns to look at her directly.

"Today a potbellied old man wearing a cowboy hat came

in to pick them up. I was there. Mr. Murray confronted him and said that if he sent in photos like that again, he would call the police."

"Was he alone?"

"Yeah, just him. Alone."

Gloria feels something akin to disappointment. A part of her wanted to meet that man, to ask him what he sees in animals that he doesn't see in people.

"Look, I also thought I saw the men from the photos with the sheep multiple times in the street. Later I realized that I was mixing them up, I was making up ideas in my head. Think about it. Millions of negatives come through the lab. It's impossible."

"Could be . . . could be. Or maybe the man in the blue suit sent the potbellied man to pick them up, right?"

Lucrecia sighs.

"Thinking like that won't get you anywhere."

The employee interrupts them. Closing time. How sad, she could've stayed there talking with Lucrecia all night. Despite eating other people's pizza crusts, she struck her as a very reasonable person. Gloria pays and they go out into the street. A gust of wind whips through their hair, the employee turns off the lights in the restaurant, and they're left under the watchful eye of a solitary streetlamp. The streets feel lonelier than before, with an air of something newly made, something untouched by anyone. Lucrecia intuits that Gloria might be thinking more clearly now that she doesn't have an empty stomach and that she's feeling afraid of walking home alone. She understands, she's been living in Queens for years. She was raped once.

"Where do you live?" she asks.

"Five blocks from here. That way," Gloria answers, gesturing toward the past and not the darkness.

"Oh, me too. Let's walk together."

Lucrecia's house is a half block away, in the opposite direction.

"Single?"

"Yes, single. I like it. I don't have to wait for anybody and nobody has to wait for me."

Gloria nods, convinced she's discovered a sensible way to live.

They've already said everything they have to say that night, so they walk in silence, but above all in peace. After a block, they stop to stare at a couple of abandoned cars, tires gnawed on by the rats. When she no longer lives there, more and more will come, they'll outnumber the humans, building their own city beneath the city.

As they start walking again, Lucrecia stumbles, a sudden dizziness, a mocking spirit. Gloria's reflexes, fine-tuned by endless games of ping-pong with her sisters, activate in time and she grabs her new friend's arm to keep her from falling to the ground. She reacts with the same speed with which she'll take me by the elbow one night in 2007, on the way to the SuperWash. In early December, after the first snowfall, I told her to be careful not to slip and I was the one who almost went flying when I stepped on the icy sidewalk, that dirty mirror in which we avoided our reflections all winter. When I hadn't yet come to keep her company, when I hadn't yet arrived in New Jersey so that together we could traverse the broken glass of that betrayal, Gloria would go to the Bergen Laundromat with a roller bag. It was a stone's throw from the small studio she'd moved into to regroup a few months before, but after the story she told me, I begged her to find somewhere else to do her laundry.

Negrito, you'll never guess what happened to me the other day, that's the line she always uses to begin her stories, no matter how dramatic or amusing. Generally, they have to do with one of her moments of intimacy with strangers. One day, a man came up to me while I was doing laundry. She'll never stop using the English word *laundry* just as she'll never stop using *subway* to refer to the metro. She told me that he listed from one side to the other and suddenly dropped the military duffel he was carrying at her feet. Wash it for me, he said in Spanish. He must have been about fifty and was very small, like a jockey. He barely came up to her chest. She ignored him and continued her folding. The man stood there, staring at his pointed, salsa-dancer shoes. The right and then the left, right, left, until he remembered what he was there for and repeated the order, this time with an authoritative tone: Wash it for me! Gloria had finished folding her clothes and was ready to go. She waited a few seconds, studying him out of the corner of her eye. She heard him start to snore. Then he let out a clicking sound and shut down completely. The little man had fallen asleep standing up, enveloped in the stench of rum, his chin stuck to his chest. She walked silently past him and out the door. But you know what, Negrito? I felt really bad and, after half a block, I went back. He must've taken a couple steps because he was closer to the washers. She moved him the way you move a piece of furniture, or in this case, a doll. With a little difficulty, she lifted him up and got him situated on a chair. He didn't say anything, didn't even groan. She stretched out his legs, resting them on his duffel bag, she bent down and tied the bag's strap to his wrist. She considered putting his clothes in one of the machines, but she hadn't liked the way he spoke to her and besides it'd gotten dark and she would've had to wait there another hour. If he'd asked nicely, I would've helped him. Before standing up to leave, I heard him whisper: give me a kiss. I'm sure that, more than to me, he was saying it to the night.

Helping a drunk, in an empty laundromat in the New

Jersey night, in a country full of weapons. I convinced her that we should switch laundromats. You have to walk a couple more blocks into the vengeful wind coming off the Hudson, but it's a big establishment with a dry floor and no unlit corners. And most important, there's a security guard who doesn't let drunks wander in. Apparently a lot of people remember to wash their clothes when they're drunk or maybe drinking gives them the courage they need to do it.

The SuperWash machines are new and the walls are freshly painted with murals of beach scenes that we sit staring at for a long time as the washing cycle finishes. Cuba, Mexico, Puerto Rico, Colombia, all beaches in one. Plus, they give you a subscription card so you can accumulate points. There's also a vending machine with drinks and snacks, video games, a change machine, and TVs that are always playing music videos.

Since I got here, we go twice a week, Monday and Thursday. We could do it all in one day, but her aversion to dirty clothes wins out over the cold weather. Besides, the place has become our confessional. We wash, we dry, we talk, and we go to the movies, that's how we've passed the winter. We've seen a lot of movies in these three months, almost always at a theater on Kennedy Boulevard. It's missing multiple letters of its name on the marquee: MAYF IR TR LEX. Near the main screen, down in front, you can still see the organ used to accompany the projection of silent movies almost a hundred years ago. On multiple occasions we've shared the theater with a nun and a priest. We've heard them burst out laughing and confide in each other. When we leave, we eat at the same Chinese restaurant, fried rice, spring rolls, Mongolian beef. The portions are huge and there's always leftovers for my lunch the next day. You know what? I never went to the movies with him. Never. She avoids saying his name, she's barely even mentioned him, twice in November, once in December. With my father, she used to go to the movies every week. Meet me in the parking lot in five minutes, he would say to her on the phone and hang up. They snuck out of work to go to the movies, like teenage lovers. When I got a little older, I went with them. Meet us at the ticket counter in half an hour, they would say and hang up. Our little ritual, him in a suit and tie, her wearing impossible heels, and me still dressed in my school uniform, a giant bucket of popcorn between us where every so often our hands touched.

Monday through Friday, she takes a bus to Paterson, where the Noon & Midnight offices are located. They promoted her and now she's managing the entire network of warehouses in New Jersey and New York. Neither of us drives, a car would mean giving up walking and we're not ready to lose the cure for anxiety that we discovered independently when we were young and living in Manhattan. If I get bored in the studio and the temperature isn't stuck below zero, I walk the streets of North Bergen. When I got in, I bought a disposable camera at the airport, probably thinking about the pictures she took with her Kodak Instamatic before losing it at the Sandro concert. I looked at them obsessively as a child, hoping they would reveal the secrets of her life in the United States. In them appeared old buildings, street signs, intersections and avenues empty on a Sunday, some full of that silent snow that gives a new shape to things; a bunch of an elevated subway stop, probably where she met up with Tigre; around ten that were really mysterious, shot from the front seat of a moving car, that could've been taken by a detective trailing a suspect; and my favorite of all, the one where she appears sitting beside Moondog, both of them looking at the camera, traveling through time all the way to me. I never found the ones of the Twin Towers. I swear I took some while they were being built; they were covered with orange plastic. Every Saturday, we get on bus 157 and in just a half hour we are at the corner of Port Authority, allowing our lives to overlap, to intermingle, her memories from the seventies, mine of the late nineties. Last week, we went to where the towers had stood. I took a picture of a piece of the boards covering the hole they left behind. You could feel a vast emptiness on the other side, every Sunday afternoon compounded into one. She saw them when they were just being built and, decades later, witnessed their collapse from only a couple miles away, sitting in front of a TV in the stone mansion of the Jewish family who hired her as their housekeeper, a few weeks after she had returned to the United States, after the terror of the money running out and the end of a marriage that sent all of us—my siblings, my parents—careening off in different directions.

At the SuperWash, where I've learned about things like her brief addiction to Demerol, she confessed to me that her dream job was to be a hotel manager, and that's how she spent a lot of her time with those Russian Jews, who ran the East Coast fur trade. She organized breakfasts, lunches, and dinners, coordinated the work of the other employees and drivers, received and signed for packages, ordered flowers and boxes of champagne for parties, sent suits to the cleaners, and had enough time to oversee the children's homework and even to take care of Mrs. Eva. When she fell down a stairway and broke a leg, four screws, Gloria bathed her for two months. When she came home drunk from a cocktail party in New York, Gloria held her hair as she vomited in the bathroom and helped her undress before going to sleep. When she cursed her husband, Gloria listened patiently. They watched the towers fall together in the sunroom, a kind of glass-walled greenhouse, where Mrs. Eva would spend her depressive crises, days when all she would eat was a green apple. The towers burning with all the beauty and horror of destruction, as a friend said, a friend I went up to the 106th floor with, three years before they fell. We stood on the dance floor of the bar where one Boeing 747 would embed itself, setting first the building and then the world on fire.

Today is the last day I'll go with her to the SuperWash. Tomorrow I fly home, tomorrow I leave her. I've asked her to come back to Colombia, there's nothing left for her to do in North Bergen. She paid my siblings' way through university and the inheritance my grandma left her is enough for her to live in peace, but she resists in her way. With evasiveness, with excuses. I want to spend another summer in New York. One more and that's it. And the drunks? And the serpentine memory of the cave? And the loneliness? Where there's freedom, there's no abandonment, where there's freedom, absolute loneliness doesn't exist, where there's freedom, the empty rowboat rocks to the rhythm of the sea, her sparkling eyes say to me.

While the dryer cycle is finishing, I tell her I'm going outside to smoke. The snow has stopped falling and you can see new growth coming in on some trees. Before long, she appears at my side and stands there watching the smoke from my cigarette mix with the vapor of my breath, forming a dense cloud, silver in the light of the moon. Here, I want to try it. You sure, Mamá? I ask, incredulous. Yes, give it to me, and she reaches out her hand for my cigarette. I pull my hand away and hold it up. Here, c'mon, she says seriously. I think about it for a second and then pass it to her. She holds it confidently and brings it to her lips. She breathes in deeply and exhales the smoke elegantly. She's been smoking her whole life without smoking, just as she's been so many other things without having been them, the manager of a five-star hotel, the lover of the owner of a Porsche Carrera, the personal secretary of Oscar de la Renta, a daughter loved by her mother. Delicious, she says, and laughs a laugh that makes me think of a transatlantic wave breaking on an esplanade, a laugh that nothing and nobody could ever take away from her.

She takes another drag off the cigarette before passing it back to me, the filter slightly oval-shaped from the pressure of her lips, and then, amused, she softly sings *fumando espero al hombre a quien yo quiero, tras los cristales de alegres ventanales* and it's in that exact moment and not in any other that I begin to write all of this that I'm now writing.

"Adiós, Lucre, and thanks for walking me home. See you at Agfa," she says, happy to know that she's made a new friend at work and that that alone has made the pain of that day worth living.

"Yeah, I'm sure we'll see each other at lunch. And

remember, those people have to live with what they do. We don't. Forget those pictures."

"Yes, that's true. I will."

And she did, she followed Lucrecia's advice, she forgot all about them for years, until something I asked her one of those nights at the SuperWash made her remember.

She goes up to the third floor and enters the apartment, taking care not to make a sound. Josefina must already be asleep. Fortunately, she doesn't have to go to the lab the next day, she thinks as she takes off her shoes and lies down in bed. She'll make cookies and hang out in her bathrobe, there's no reason to try to talk to her father. Before closing her eyes, she visits all the people she encountered in the last twelve hours, she sees them sleeping in their beds, Amparo and her mother somewhere nearby, Carlota and Torero holding each other, Tito and his friend holding each other, Raúl, Lucrecia, the man running the pizzeria, the elegant thief on the subway. She has a thought for all of them, except for Tigre. Pretty soon, she'll fall asleep with her clothes on.

She doesn't hear the phone ring at five o'clock in the morning. A hand shakes her. It shakes her again, more forcefully, until it finally succeeds in pulling her out of sleep. She opens her eyes. It's Carlos Arturo, Josefina says in a whisper.

He tells Gloria that Tigre was walking down the sidewalk with the borrowed turntable, he crossed a street and, when he was already on the other side, almost to the corner of the building where they were waiting for him, he heard a car slam on its brakes. He turned to look. The police. One of the officers got out of the car and asked him where he was going with the turntable. *It's yours?* And of course, Tigre could only stammer a few words in English. She always had to talk for him at the bank, order his hamburgers without onion. Confronted with his stony silence, the officer insisted, this time in bad Spanish: *eres tuyo?* Nothing to be done, Tigre couldn't make himself understood. The other officer got out of the car and asked for his documents. Papers. He didn't have papers. He'd come to the United States as a tourist and his visa had expired a long time ago. They're going to deport him. He's in a cell right now; Carlos Arturo says goodbye with those words.

Walking to her room, she remembers that trip to Niagara Falls when she met him, after signing up for the tour they were offering. They stopped in a vacant lot to stretch their legs, beside a couple elm trees. It was such nice weather that Gloria and Tigre decided to take a little walk, talking and studying each other out of the corners of their eyes. My first love, my first sorrow, she says to me, smiling.

Apollo 13 would never land on the moon. Sandro would get fat and she would never again wait for Tigre in La Mallorquina diner nor in any other. Two days later, they put him on a plane. If she'd been direct family, she would've been the one and not his cousin who would've taken him his fishing pole; that's all he asked to have brought to him in his cell before they repatriated him. In Colombia, he would die within a few months from lymphatic cancer and all that would be left of him was his nickname and the memory of some tears that Gloria would never see again.

She doesn't yet know what it is she feels, it'll take her weeks, months to understand. For now, she gets back in bed. When she does, she hears something rustle in one of her skirt pockets, a piece of paper. She takes it out. It's the page from the magazine. She unfolds it and decides to read the end of the article. She only had one paragraph left. To date, Moondog has put out six albums, he's invented many instruments, and he's friends with multiple prominent jazz musicians. She also learns that his fame spread far beyond Manhattan when a well-known singer recorded one of his songs: "All Is Loneliness."

She folds the page carefully and puts it back in her pocket. She always goes through her pockets before putting any clothes in the washer, so she won't lose it. The light is starting to slip softly in through the window. Pretty soon a cat or a drunk will knock over a bottle. All is loneliness. She likes it. That morning, it tastes like the truth. The only possible truth. A truth that she'll lose along the way and will have to rediscover, a truth radically different from any idea of social isolation and a long way from being a lament. A truth like the sky. From that day onward, the day when Gloria was Gloria for the first time, she'll make it her own. She'll repeat it to herself in secret like a personal prayer and it'll help her forget, among other things, Tigre.

She crosses her hands over her stomach and stares at the ceiling. She thinks that the next time she sees Moondog on Sixth Avenue, she'll ask him if they can write a song together. A song called: "This Is Where Words Die."

ANDRÉS FELIPE SOLANO is the author of the novels *Sálvame, Joe Louis, Los hermanos Cuervo,* and *Cementerios de neón.* He also published "Salario mínimo," an essay about his experience as a factory worker for six months. *Corea, apuntes desde la cuerda floja,* a nonfiction book about his life in South Korea, received the 2016 Premio Biblioteca de Narrativa Colombiana and was translated into Korean in 2018. His work has appeared in *The New York Times Magazine, McSweeney's, Words Without Borders,* and *Freeman's.* He was featured in *Granta 113: The Best of Young Spanish-Language Novelists.* He currently lives in Seoul.

© Luisa Rivera

WILL VANDERHYDEN is an award-winning translator who has translated several books for Open Letter, Deep Vellum, and Akashic.